She was blond and beautiful and bewildered.

Her hair was wet and straight as the rain. Her face—though it could have used some color—was delicate as a fairy's.

"Excuse me." Her voice sounded rusty, as if she hadn't used it in days. "Are you Mr. Parris?"

There was one blinding moment when he couldn't seem to speak. And the only thought that came to his mind was *There you are, finally. What the hell took you so long?*

He struggled to put on a bland investigator's expression. "Yeah." Whatever that first absurd, unprecedented reaction was, she was still a potential client. And surely no dame who had ever walked through Sam Spade's hallowed door had ever been more perfect.

She'd ruined her suit and designer shoes in the rain, and the canvas bag she clutched with both hands looked intriguingly out of place.

Damsel in distress, he mused, and his lips curved. Just what the doctor ordered.

Dear Reader,

Any month with a new Nora Roberts book *has* to be special, and this month is *extra* special, because this book is the first of a wonderful new trilogy. *Hidden Star* begins THE STARS OF MITHRA, three stories about strong heroines, wonderful heroes—and three gems destined to bring them together. The adventure begins for Bailey James with the loss of her memory—and the entrance of coolheaded (well, until he sees *her*) private eye Cade Parris into her life. He wants to believe in her—not to mention love her—but what is she doing with a sackful of cash and a diamond the size of a baby's fist?

It's a month for miniseries, with Marilyn Pappano revisiting her popular SOUTHERN KNIGHTS with *Convincing Jamey*, and Alicia Scott continuing MAXIMILLIAN'S CHILDREN with *MacNamara's Woman*. Not to mention the final installment of Beverly Bird's THE WEDDING RING, *Saving Susannah*, and the second book of Marilyn Tracy's ALMOST, TEXAS miniseries, *Almost a Family*.

Finally, welcome Intimate Moments' newest author, Maggie Price. She's part of our WOMEN TO WATCH cross-line promotion, with each line introducing a brand-new author to you. In *Prime Suspect*, Maggie spins an irresistible tale about a by-the-book detective falling for a suspect, a beautiful criminal profiler who just may be in over her head. As an aside, you might like to know that Maggie herself once worked as a crime analyst for the Oklahoma City police department.

So enjoy all these novels—and then be sure to come back next month for more of the best romance reading around, right here in Silhouette Intimate Moments.

Yours,

Senior Editor and Editorial Coordinator

Nora Roberts

HIDDEN STAR

The Stars of Mithra

Published by Silhouette Books

America's Publisher of Contemporary Romance

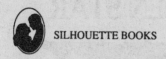

SILHOUETTE BOOKS

ISBN 0-373-07811-0

HIDDEN STAR

Copyright © 1997 by Nora Roberts

This edition published by arrangement with Harlequin Books S.A.

® and TM are trademarks of Harlequin Books S.A., used under license.
Trademarks indicated with ® are registered in the United States Patent
and Trademark Office, the Canadian Trade Marks Office and in other
countries.

Printed in U.S.A.

NORA ROBERTS

is one of Silhouette Books' most popular and prolific authors, as well as a *New York Times* bestseller in both hardcover and paperback. Nora was the first author inducted into the Romance Writers of America's Hall of Fame and has received awards for her fiction, her creativity, her sales and her contribution to the genre. She has received lifetime achievement awards from the Romance Writers of America, Waldenbooks and *Romantic Times* magazine, and bestselling title and series awards from booksellers, readers and peers.

Nora Roberts is a consummate storyteller. She is known for her humor, creativity and willingness to take chances. Nora's commitment to her characters, to her writing and, most especially, to her readers has earned her fans all over the world.

To white knights and their damsels

Chapter 1

Cade Parris wasn't having the best of days when the woman of his dreams walked into his office. His secretary had quit the day before—not that she'd been much of a prize anyway, being more vigilant about her manicure than maintaining the phone logs. But he needed someone to keep track of things and shuffle papers into files. Even the raise he offered out of sheer desperation hadn't swayed her to give up her sudden determination to become a country-and-western singing sensation.

So his secretary was heading off to Nashville in a second-hand pickup, and his office looked like the ten miles of bad road he sincerely hoped she traveled.

She hadn't exactly had her mind on her work the past month or two. That impression had been more than confirmed when he fished a bologna sandwich out of the file drawer. At least he thought the blob in the plastic bag was bologna. And it had been filed under *L*—for Lunch?

He didn't bother to swear, nor did he bother to answer the phone that rang incessantly on the empty desk in his reception area. He had reports to type up, and as typing wasn't one of his finer skills, he just wanted to get on with it.

Parris Investigations wasn't what some would call a thriving enterprise. But it suited him, just as the cluttered two-room office squeezed into the top floor of a narrow brick building with bad plumbing in North West D.C. suited him.

He didn't need plush carpets or polished edges. He'd grown up with all that, with the pomp and pretenses, and had had his fill of it all by the time he reached the age of twenty. Now, at thirty, with one bad marriage behind him and a family who continued to be baffled by his pursuits, he was, by and large, a contented man.

He had his investigator's license, a decent reputation as a man who got the job done, and enough income to keep his agency well above water.

Though actual business income was a bit of a problem just then. He was in what he liked to call a lull. Most of his caseload consisted of insurance and domestic work—a few steps down from the thrills he'd imagined when he set out to become a private investigator. He'd just cleaned up two cases, both of them minor insurance frauds that hadn't taken much effort or innovation to close.

He had nothing else coming in, his greedy blood-sucker of a landlord was bumping up his rent, the engine in his car had been making unsettling noises lately, his air conditioner was on the fritz. And the roof was leaking again.

He took the spindly yellow-leafed philodendron his double-crossing secretary had left behind and set it on the uncarpeted floor under the steady drip, hoping it might drown.

He could hear a voice droning into his answering machine. It was his mother's voice. Lord, he thought, did a man ever really escape his mother?

"Cade, dear, I hope you haven't forgotten the Embassy Ball. You know you're to escort Pamela Lovett. I had lunch with her aunt today, and she tells me that Pamela just looks marvelous after her little sojourn to Monaco."

"Yeah, yeah, yeah," he muttered, and narrowed his eyes at the computer. He and machines had poor and untrusting relationships.

He sat down and faced the screen as his mother continued to chatter: "Have you had your tux cleaned? Do make time to get a haircut, you looked so scraggly the last time I saw you."

And don't forget to wash behind the ears, he thought sourly, and tuned her out. She was never going to accept that the Parris life-style wasn't his life-style, that he just didn't want to lunch at the club or squire bored former debutantes around Washington and that his opinion wasn't going to change by dint of her persuasion.

He'd wanted adventure, and though struggling to type up a report on some poor slob's fake whiplash wasn't exactly Sam Spade territory, he was doing the job.

Mostly he didn't feel useless or bored or out of place. He liked the sound of traffic outside his window, even though the window was only open because the building and its scum-sucking landlord didn't go in for central air-conditioning and his unit was broken. The heat was intense, and the rain was coming in, but with the window closed, the offices would have been as airless and stifling as a tomb.

Sweat rolled down his back, making him itchy and irritable. He was stripped down to a T-shirt and jeans, his long fingers fumbling a bit on the computer keys. He had to shovel his hair out of his face several times, which ticked him off. His mother was right. He needed a haircut.

So when it got in the way again, he ignored it, as he ignored the sweat, the heat, the buzz of traffic, the steady drip from the ceiling. He sat, methodically punching a key at a time, a remarkably handsome man with a scowl on his face.

He'd inherited the Parris looks—the clever green eyes that could go broken-bottle sharp or as soft as sea mist, depending on his mood. The hair that needed a trim was dark mink brown and tended to wave. Just now, it curled at his neck, over his ears, and was beginning to annoy him. His nose was straight, aristocratic and a little long, his mouth firm and quick to smile when he was amused. And to sneer when he wasn't.

Though his face had become more honed since the embarrassing cherubic period of his youth and early adolescence, it still sported dimples. He was looking forward to middle age, when, with luck, they'd become manly creases.

He'd wanted to be rugged, and instead was stuck with the slick, dreamy good looks of a *GQ* cover—for one of which he'd posed in his middle twenties, under protest and great family pressure.

The phone rang again. This time he heard his sister's voice, haranguing him about missing some lame cocktail party in honor of some big-bellied senator she was endorsing.

He thought about just ripping the damn answering machine out of the wall and heaving it, and his sister's nagging voice, out the window into the traffic on Wisconsin Avenue.

Then the rain that was only adding to the miserably thick heat began to drip on the top of his head. The computer blinked off, for no reason he could see other than sheer nastiness, and the coffee he'd forgotten he was heating boiled over with a spiteful hiss.

He leaped up, burned his hand on the pot. He swore viciously as the pot smashed, shattering glass, and spewing hot coffee in all directions. He ripped open a drawer, grabbed for a stack of napkins and sliced his thumb with the lethal edge of his former—and now thoroughly damned to perdition—secretary's nail file.

When the woman walked in, he was still cursing and bleeding and had just tripped over the philodendron set in the middle of the floor and didn't even look up.

It was hardly a wonder she simply stood there, damp from the rain, her face pale as death and her eyes wide with shock.

"Excuse me." Her voice sounded rusty, as if she hadn't used it in days. "I must have the wrong office." She inched backward, and those big, wide brown eyes shifted to the name printed on the door. She hesitated, then looked back at him. "Are you Mr. Parris?"

There was a moment, one blinding moment, when he couldn't seem to speak. He knew he was staring at her, couldn't help himself. His heart simply stood still. His knees went weak. And the only thought that came to his mind was *There you are, finally. What the hell took you so long?*

And because that was so ridiculous, he struggled to put a bland, even cynical, investigator's expression on his face.

"Yeah." He remembered the handkerchief in his pocket, and wrapped it over his busily bleeding thumb. "Just had a little accident here."

"I see." Though she didn't appear to, the way she continued to stare at his face. "I've come at a bad time. I don't have an appointment. I thought maybe…"

"Looks like my calendar's clear."

He wanted her to come in, all the way in. Whatever

that first absurd, unprecedented reaction of his, she was still a potential client. And surely no dame who ever walked through Sam Spade's hallowed door had ever been more perfect.

She was blond and beautiful and bewildered. Her hair was wet, sleek down to her shoulders and straight as the rain. Her eyes were bourbon brown, in a face that—though it could have used some color—was delicate as a fairy's. It was heart-shaped, the cheeks a gentle curve and the mouth was full, unpainted and solemn.

She'd ruined her suit and shoes in the rain. He recognized both as top-quality, that quietly exclusive look found only in designer salons. Against the wet blue silk of her suit, the canvas bag she clutched with both hands looked intriguingly out of place.

Damsel in distress, he mused, and his lips curved. Just what the doctor ordered.

"Why don't you come in, close the door, Miss…?"

Her heart bumped twice, hammer-hard, and she tightened her grip on the bag. "You're a private investigator?"

"That's what it says on the door." Cade smiled again, ruthlessly using the dimples while he watched her gnaw that lovely lower lip. Damned if he wouldn't like to gnaw on it himself.

And that response, he thought with a little relief, was a lot more like it. Lust was a feeling he could understand.

"Let's go back to my office." He surveyed the

damage—broken glass, potting soil, pools of coffee. "I think I'm finished in here for now."

"All right." She took a deep breath, stepped in, then closed the door. She supposed she had to start somewhere.

Picking her way over the debris, she followed him into the adjoining room. It was furnished with little more than a desk and a couple of bargain-basement chairs. Well, she couldn't be choosy about decor, she reminded herself. She waited until he'd sat behind his desk, tipped back in his chair and smiled at her again in that quick, trust-me way.

"Do you— Could I—" She squeezed her eyes tight, centered herself again. "Do you have some credentials I could see?"

More intrigued, he took out his license, handed it to her. She wore two very lovely rings, one on each hand, he noticed. One was a square-cut citrine in an antique setting, the other a trio of colored stones. Her earrings matched the second ring, he noted when she tucked her hair behind her ear and studied his license as if weighing each printed word.

"Would you like to tell me what the problem is, Miss...?"

"I think—" She handed him back his license, then gripped the bag two-handed again. "I think I'd like to hire you." Her eyes were on his face again, as intently, as searchingly, as they had been on the license. "Do you handle missing-persons cases?"

Who did you lose, sweetheart? he wondered. He hoped, for her sake and for the sake of the nice little fantasy that was building in his head, it wasn't a husband. "Yeah, I handle missing persons."

"Your, ah, rate?"

"Two-fifty a day, plus expenses." When she nodded, he slid over a legal pad, picked up a pencil. "Who do you want me to find?"

She took a long, shuddering breath. "Me. I need you to find me."

Watching her, he tapped the pencil against the pad. "Looks like I already have. You want me to bill you, or do you want to pay now?"

"No." She could feel it cracking. She'd held on so long—or at least it seemed so long—but now she could feel that branch she'd gripped when the world dropped out from under her begin to crack. "I don't remember. Anything. I don't—" Her voice began to hitch. She took her hands off the bag in her lap to press them to her face. "I don't know who I am. I don't know who I am." And then she was weeping the words into her hands. "I don't know who I am."

Cade had a lot of experience with hysterical women. He'd grown up with females who used flowing tears and gulping sobs as the answer to anything from a broken nail to a broken marriage. So he rose from his desk, armed himself with a box of tissues and crouched in front of her.

"Here now, sweetheart. Don't worry. It's going to be just fine." With gentle expertise, he mopped at her face as he spoke. He patted her hand, stroked her hair, studied her swimming eyes.

"I'm sorry. I can't—"

"Just cry it out," he told her. "You'll feel better for it." Rising, he went into the closet-size bathroom and poured her a paper cup of water.

When she had a lapful of damp tissues and three crushed paper cups, she let out a little jerky sigh. "I'm sorry. Thank you. I do feel better." Her cheeks pinkened a bit with embarrassment as she gathered up the tissues and mangled cups. Cade took them from her, dumped them in the wastebasket, then rested a hip on the corner of his desk.

"You want to tell me about it now?"

She nodded, then linked her fingers and began to twist them together. "I— There isn't that much to tell. I just don't remember anything. Who I am, what I do, where I'm from. Friends, family. Nothing." Her breath caught again, and she released it slowly. "Nothing," she repeated.

It was a dream come true, he thought, the beautiful woman without a past coming out of the rain and into his office. He flicked a glance at the bag she still held in her lap. They'd get to that in a minute. "Why don't you tell me the first thing you do remember?"

"I woke up in a room—a little hotel on Sixteenth Street." Letting her head rest back against the chair, she closed her eyes and tried to bring things into focus. "Even that's unclear. I was curled up on the bed, and there was a chair propped under the doorknob. It was raining. I could hear the rain. I was groggy and disoriented, but my heart was pounding so hard, as if I'd wakened from a nightmare. I still had my shoes on. I remember wondering why I'd gone to bed with my shoes on. The room was dim and stuffy. All the windows were closed. I was so tired, logy, so I went into the bathroom to splash water on my face.''

Now she opened her eyes, looked into his. "I saw my face in the mirror. This ugly little mirror with black splotches where it needed to be resilvered. And it meant nothing to me. The face." She lifted a hand, ran it over her cheek, her jaw. "My face meant nothing to me. I couldn't remember the name that went with the face, or the thoughts or the plans or the past. I didn't know how I'd gotten to that horrid room. I looked through the drawers and the closet, but there was nothing. No clothes. I was afraid to stay there, but I didn't know where to go."

"The bag? Was that all you had with you?"

"Yes." Her hand clutched at the straps again. "No purse, no wallet, no keys. This was in my pocket." She reached into the pocket of her jacket and took out a small scrap of notepaper.

Cade took it from her, skimmed the quick scrawling writing.

Bailey, Sat at 7, right? MJ

"I don't know what it means. I saw a newspaper. Today's Friday."

"Mmm. Write it down," Cade said, handing her a pad and pen.

"What?"

"Write down what it says on the note."

"Oh." Gnawing her lip again, she complied.

Though he didn't have to compare the two to come to his conclusions, he took the pad from her, set it and the note side by side. "Well, you're not M.J., so I'd say you're Bailey."

She blinked, swallowed. "What?"

"From the look of M.J.'s writing, he or she's a lefty. You're right-handed. You've got neat, simple penmanship, M.J.'s got an impatient scrawl. The note was in your pocket. Odds are you're Bailey."

"Bailey." She tried to absorb the name, the hope of it, the feel and taste of identity. But it was dry and unfamiliar. "It doesn't mean anything."

"It means we have something to call you, and someplace to start. Tell me what you did next."

Distracted she blinked at him. "Oh, I... There was a phone book in the room. I looked up detective agencies."

"Why'd you pick mine?"

"The name. It sounded strong." She managed her first smile, and though it was weak, it was there. "I started to call, but then I thought I might get put off, and if I just showed up... So I waited in the room until it was office hours, then I walked for a little while, then I got a cab. And here I am."

"Why didn't you go to a hospital? Call a doctor?"

"I thought about it." She looked down at her hands. "I just didn't."

She was leaving out big chunks, he mused. Going around his desk, he opened a drawer, pulled out a candy bar. "You didn't say anything about stopping for breakfast." He watched her study the candy he offered with puzzlement and what appeared to be amusement. "This'll hold you until we can do better."

"Thank you." With neat, precise movements, she unwrapped the chocolate bar. Maybe part of the fluttering in her stomach was hunger. "Mr. Parris, I may have people worried about me. Family, friends. I may have a child. I don't know." Her eyes deepened, fixed on a point over his shoulder. "I don't think I do. I can't believe anyone could forget her own child. But people may be worried, wondering what happened to me. Why I didn't come home last night."

"You could have gone to the police."

"I didn't want to go to the police." This time, her voice was clipped, definite. "Not until... No, I don't want to involve the police." She wiped her fingers on a fresh tissue, then began to tear it into strips. "Someone may be looking for me who isn't a friend, who isn't family. Who isn't concerned with my well-being. I don't know why I feel that way, I only know I'm afraid. It's more than just not remembering. But I can't understand anything, any of it, until I know who I am."

Maybe it was those big, soft, moist eyes staring up at him, or the damsel-in-distress nerves of her restless hands. Either way, he couldn't resist showing off, just a little.

"I can tell you a few things already. You're an intelligent woman, early-to-mid-twenties. You have a good eye for color and style, and enough of a bankroll to indulge it with Italian shoes and silk suits. You're neat, probably organized. You prefer the understated to the obvious. Since you don't evade well, I'd say you're an equally poor liar. You've got a good head on your shoulders, you think things through. You don't panic easily. And you like chocolate.''

She balled the empty candy wrapper in her hand. "Why do you assume all that?"

"You speak well, even when you're frightened. You thought about how you were going to handle this and went through all the steps, logically. You dress well—quality over flair. You have a good manicure, but no flashy polish. Your jewelry is unique, interesting, but not ornate. And you've been holding back information since you walked through the door because you haven't decided yet how much you're going to trust me."

"How much should I trust you?"

"You came to me."

She acknowledged that, rose and walked to his window. The rain drummed, underscoring the vague headache that hovered just behind her eyes. "I don't recognize the city," she murmured. "Yet I feel I should. I know where I am, because I saw a newspaper, the *Washington Post*. I know what the White House and the Capitol look like. I know the monuments—but I could have seen them on television, or in a book."

Though it was wet from incoming rain, she rested her hands on the sill, appreciated the coolness there. "I feel as though I dropped out of nowhere into that ugly hotel room. Still, I know how to read and write and walk and talk. The cabdriver had the radio on, and I recognized music. I recognized trees. I wasn't surprised that rain was wet. I smelled burned coffee when I came in, and it wasn't an unfamiliar odor. I know your eyes are green. And when the rain clears, I know the sky will be blue."

She sighed once. "So I didn't drop out of nowhere. There are things I know, things I'm sure of. But my own face means nothing to me, and what's behind the face is blank. I may have hurt someone, done something. I may be selfish and calculating, even cruel. I may have a husband I cheat on or neighbors I've alienated."

She turned back then, and her face was tight and set, a tough contrast to the fragility of lashes still wet from tears. "I don't know if I'm going to like who you find when you find me, Mr. Parris, but I need to know." She set the bag on his desk, hesitated briefly, then opened it. "I think I have enough to meet your fee."

He came from money, the kind that aged and increased and propagated over generations. But even with his background, he'd never seen so much in one place at one time. The canvas bag was filled with wrapped stacks of hundred-dollar bills—all crisp and clean. Fascinated, Cade took out a stack, flipped through. Yes, indeed, he mused, every one of the bills had Ben Franklin's homely and dignified face.

"I'd have to guess about a million," he murmured.

"One million, two hundred thousand." Bailey shuddered as she looked into the bag. "I counted the

stacks. I don't know where I got it or why I had it
with me. I may have stolen it.''

Tears began to swim again as she turned away. ''It
could be ransom money. I could be involved in a
kidnapping. There could be a child somewhere, being
held, and I've taken the ransom money. I just—''

''Let's add a vivid imagination to those other qual-
ities.''

It was the cool and casual tone of his voice that
had her turning back. ''There's a fortune in there.''

''A million two isn't much of a fortune these
days.'' He dropped the money back in the bag. ''And
I'm sorry, Bailey, you just don't fit the cold, calculating kidnapper type.''

''But you can check. You can find out, discreetly,
if there's been an abduction.''

''Sure. If the cops are involved, I can get something.''

''And if there's been a murder?'' Struggling to stay
calm, she reached into the bag again. This time she
took out a .38.

A cautious man, Cade nudged the barrel aside, took
it from her. It was a Smith and Wesson, and at his
quick check, he discovered it was fully loaded.
''How'd this feel in your hand?''

''I don't understand.''

''How'd it feel when you picked it up? The weight,
the shape?''

Though she was baffled by the question, she did
her best to answer thoroughly. ''Not as heavy as I
thought it should. It seemed that something that had

that kind of power would have more weight, more substance. I suppose it felt awkward.''

''The pen didn't.''

This time she simply dragged her hands through her hair. ''I don't know what you're talking about. I've just shown you over a million dollars and a gun. You're talking about pens.''

''When I handed you a pen to write, it didn't feel awkward. You didn't have to think about it. You just took it and used it.'' He smiled a little and slipped the gun into his pocket, instead of the bag. ''I think you're a lot more accustomed to holding a pen than a .38 special.''

There was some relief in that, the simple logic of it. But it didn't chase away all the clouds. ''Maybe you're right. It doesn't mean I didn't use it.''

''No, it doesn't. And since you've obviously put your hands all over it, we can't prove you didn't. I can check and see if it's registered and to whom.''

Her eyes lit with hope. ''It could be mine.'' She reached out, took his hand, squeezed it in a gesture that was thoughtless and natural. ''We'd have a name then. I'd know my name then. I didn't realize it could be so simple.''

''It may be simple.''

''You're right.'' She released his hand, began to pace. Her movements were smooth, controlled. ''I'm getting ahead of myself. But it helps so much you see, so much more than I imagined, just to tell someone. Someone who knows how to figure things out. I don't know if I'm very good at puzzles. Mr. Parris—"

"Cade," he said, intrigued that he could find her economical movements so sexy. "Let's keep it simple."

"Cade." She drew in a breath, let it out. "It's nice to call someone by name. You're the only person I know, the only person I remember having a conversation with. I can't tell you how odd that is, and, right now, how comforting."

"Why don't we make me the first person you remember having a meal with? One candy bar isn't much of a breakfast. You look worn out, Bailey."

It was so odd to hear him use that name when he looked at her. Because it was all she had, she struggled to respond to it. "I'm tired," she admitted. "It doesn't feel as if I've slept very much. I don't know when I've eaten last."

"How do you feel about scrambled eggs?"

The smile wisped around her mouth again. "I haven't the faintest idea."

"Well, let's find out." He started to pick up the canvas bag, but she laid a hand over his on the straps.

"There's something else." She didn't speak for a moment, but kept her eyes on his, as she had when she first walked in. Searching, measuring, deciding. But there was, she knew, really no choice. He was all she had. "Before I show you, I need to ask for a promise."

"You hire me, Bailey, I work for you."

"I don't know if what I'm going to ask is com-

pletely ethical, but I still need your word. If during
the course of your investigation you discover that I've
committed a crime, I need your word that you'll find
out everything you can, all the circumstances, all the
facts, before you turn me over to the police.''

He angled his head. ''You assume I'll turn you in.''

''If I've broken the law, I'll expect you to turn me
over to the police. But I need all the reasons before
you do. I need to understand all the whys, the hows,
the who. Will you give me your word on that?''

''Sure.'' He took the hand she held out. It was delicate as porcelain, steady as a rock. And she, he
thought, whoever she was, was a fascinating combination of the fragile and the steely. ''No cops until
we know all of it. You can trust me, Bailey.''

''You're trying to make me comfortable with the
name.'' Again, without thinking, in a move that was
as innate as the color of her eyes, she kissed his
cheek. ''You're very kind.''

Kind enough, she thought, that he would hold her
now if she asked. And she so desperately wanted to
be held, soothed, to be promised that her world would
snap back into focus again at any moment. But she
needed to stand on her own. She could only hope she
was the kind of woman who stood on her own feet
and faced her own problems.

''There's one more thing.'' She turned to the canvas bag again, slid her hand deep inside, felt for the
thick velvet pouch, the weight of what was snugged
inside it. ''I think it's probably the most important
thing.''

She drew it out and very carefully, with what he thought of as reverence, untied the pouch and slid its contents into the cup of her palm.

The money had surprised him, the gun had concerned him. But this awed him. The gleam of it, the regal glint, even in the rain-darkened room, held a stunning and sumptuous power.

The gem filled the palm of her hand, its facets clean and sharp enough to catch even the faintest flicker of light and shoot it into the air in bright, burning lances. It belonged, he thought, on the crown of a mythical queen, or lying heavily between the breasts of some ancient goddess.

"I've never seen a sapphire that big."

"It isn't a sapphire." And when she passed it to his hand, she would have sworn she felt the exchange of heat. "It's a blue diamond, somewhere around a hundred carats. Brilliant-cut, most likely from Asia Minor. There are no inclusions visible to the naked eye, and it is rare in both color and size. I'd have to guess its market worth at easily three times the amount of money in the bag."

He wasn't looking at the gem any longer, but at her. When she lifted her eyes to his, she shook her head. "I don't know how I know. But I do. Just as I know it's not all...it's not...complete."

"What do you mean?"

"I wish I knew. But it's too strong a feeling, an almost-recognition. I know the stone is only part of the whole. Just as I know it can't possibly belong to me. It doesn't really belong to anyone. Any one," she repeated, separating the word into two. "I must have stolen it."

She pressed her lips together, lifted her chin, squared her shoulders. "I might have killed for it."

Chapter 2

Cade took her home. It was the best option he could
think of, tucking her away. And he wanted that canvas bag and its contents in his safe as quickly as possible. She hadn't argued when he led her out of the
building, had made no comment about the sleek little
Jag parked in the narrow spot on the cracked asphalt
lot.

He preferred using his nondescript and well-dented
sedan for his work, but until it was out of the shop,
he was stuck with the streamlined, eye-catching Jag-
uar.

But she said nothing, not even when he drove into
a lovely old neighborhood with graceful shade trees
and tidy flower-trimmed lawns and into the driveway
of a dignified Federal-style brick house.

He'd been prepared to explain that he'd inherited

it from a great-aunt who had a soft spot for him—which was true enough. And that he lived there because he liked the quiet and convenience of the established neighborhood in the heart of Washington.

But she didn't ask.

It seemed to Cade that she'd simply run down. Whatever energy had pushed her into going out in the rain, seeking his office and telling her story had drained out, leaving her listless.

And fragile again. He had to check the urge to simply gather her up and carry her inside. He could imagine it clearly—the stalwart knight, my lady's champion, carrying her into the safety of the castle and away from any and all dragons that plagued her.

He really had to stop thinking things like that.

Instead, he hefted the canvas bag, took her unresisting hand and led her through the graceful foyer, down the hall and directly into the kitchen.

"Scrambled eggs," he said, pulling out a chair for her and nudging her down to sit at the pedestal table.

"All right. Yes. Thank you."

She felt limp, unfocused, and terribly grateful to him. He wasn't peppering her with questions, nor had he looked particularly shocked or appalled by her story. Perhaps it was the nature of his business that made him take it all in stride, but whatever the reason, she was thankful for the time he was giving her to recoup.

Now he was moving around the kitchen in a casual, competent manner. Breaking brown eggs in a white bowl, popping bread in a toaster that sat on a granite-colored counter. She should offer to help, she thought. It seemed the right thing to do. But she was so dreadfully tired, and it was so pleasant to just sit in the big kitchen with rain drumming musically on the roof and watch him handle the simple task of making breakfast.

He was taking care of her. And she was letting him. Bailey closed her eyes and wondered if she was the kind of woman who needed to be tended to by a man, who enjoyed the role of the helpless female.

She hoped not, almost fiercely hoped not. Then wondered why such a minor, insignificant personality trait should matter so much, when she couldn't be sure she wasn't a thief or murderer.

She caught herself studying her hands, wondering about them. Short, neat, rounded nails coated in clear polish. Did that mean she was practical? The hands were soft, uncallused. It was doubtful she worked with them, pursued manual labor of any kind.

The rings... Very pretty, not bold so much as unique. At least it seemed they were. She knew the stones that winked back at her. Garnet, citrine, amethyst. How could she know the names of colored stones and not know the name of her closest friend?

Did she have any friends?

Was she a kind person or a catty one, generous or a faultfinder? Did she laugh easily and cry at sad movies? Was there a man she loved who loved her?

Had she stolen more than a million dollars and used that ugly little gun?

She jolted when Cade set her plate in front of her, then settled when he laid a hand on her shoulder.

"You need to eat." He went back to the stove, brought the cup he'd left there. "And I think tea's a better bet than coffee."

"Yes. Thank you." She picked up her fork, scooped up some eggs, tasted. "I like them." She managed a smile again, a hesitant, shy smile that touched his heart. "That's something."

He sat across from her with his mug of coffee. "I'm known throughout the civilized world for my scrambled eggs."

Her smile steadied, bloomed. "I can see why. The little dashes of dill and paprika are inspired."

"Wait till you taste my Spanish omelets."

"Master of the egg." She continued to eat, comforted by the easy warmth she felt between them. "Do you cook a lot?"

She glanced around the kitchen. Stone-colored cabinets and warm, light wood. An uncurtained window over a double sink of white porcelain. Coffeemaker, toaster, jumbled sections of the morning paper.

The room was neat, she observed, but not obsessively so. And it was a marked contrast to the clutter and mess of his office. "I never asked if you were married."

"Divorced, and I cook when I'm tired of eating out."

"I wonder what I do—eat out or cook."

"You recognized paprika and dill when you tasted them." Leaning back, he sipped his coffee and studied her. "You're beautiful." Her gaze flicked up, startled and, he noted, instantly wary. "Just an observation, Bailey. We have to work with what we know. You are beautiful—it's quiet, understated, nothing that seems particularly contrived or enhanced. You don't go for the flashy, and you don't take a compliment on your looks casually. In fact, I've just made you very nervous."

She picked up her cup, held it in both hands. "Are you trying to?"

"No, but it's interesting and sweet—the way you blush and eye me suspiciously at the same time. You can relax, I'm not hitting on you." But it was a thought, he admitted, a fascinating and arousing thought. "I don't think you're a pushover, either," he continued. "I doubt a man would get very far with you just by telling you that you have eyes like warm brandy, and that the contrast between them and that cool, cultured voice packs a hell of a sexual impact."

She lifted her cup and, though it took an effort, kept her gaze level with his. "It sounds very much like you're hitting on me."

His dimples flashed with charm when he grinned. "See, not a pushover. But polite, very polite and well mannered. There's New England in your voice, Bailey."

Staring, she lowered the cup again. "New England?"

"Connecticut, Massachusetts—I'm not sure. But there's a whiff of Yankee society upbringing in your voice, especially when it turns cold."

"New England." She strained for a connection, some small link. "It doesn't mean anything to me."

"It gives me another piece to work with. You've got class written all over you. You were born with it, or you developed it, either way it's there." He rose, took her plate. "And so's the exhaustion. You need to sleep."

"Yes." The thought of going back to that hotel room had her forcing back a shudder. "Should I call your office, set up another appointment? I wrote down the number of the hotel and room where I'm staying. You could call me if you find anything."

"You're not going back there." He had her hand again, drew her to her feet and began to lead her out of the kitchen. "You can stay here. There's plenty of room."

"Here?"

"I think it's best if you're where I can keep an eye on you, at least for the time being." Back in the foyer, he led her up the stairs. "It's a safe, quiet neighborhood, and until we figure out how you got your hands on a million two and a diamond as big as your fist, I don't want you wandering the streets."

"You don't know me."

"Neither do you. That's something else we're going to work on."

He opened the door to a room where the dim light flickered quietly through lace curtains onto a polished oak floor. A little seating area of button-back chairs and a piecrust table was arranged in front of a fireplace where a fern thrived in the hearth. A wedding-ring quilt was spread over a graceful four poster, plumped invitingly with pillows.

"Take a nap," he advised. "There's a bath through there, and I'll dig up something for you to change into after you've rested."

She felt the tears backing up again, scoring her throat with a mixture of fear and gratitude and outrageous fatigue. "Do you invite all your clients into your home as houseguests?"

"No." He touched her cheek and, because he wanted to gather her close, feel how her head would settle on his shoulder, dropped his hand again. "Just the ones who need it. I'm going to be downstairs. I've got some things to do."

"Cade." She reached for his hand, held it a moment. "Thank you. It looks like I picked the right name out of the phone book."

"Get some sleep. Let me do the worrying for a while."

"I will. Don't close the door," she said quickly when he stepped out into the hall.

He pushed it open again, studied her standing there in the patterned light, looking so delicate, so lost. "I'll be right downstairs."

She listened to his footsteps recede before sinking down on the padded bench at the foot of the bed. It might be foolish to trust him, to put her life in his hands as completely as she had. But she did trust him. Not only because her world consisted only of him and what she'd told him, but because every instinct inside her told her this was a man she could depend on.

Perhaps it was just blind faith and desperate hope, but at the moment she didn't think she could survive another hour without both. So her future depended on Cade Parris, on his ability to handle her present and his skill in unearthing her past.

She slipped off her shoes, took off her jacket and folded it on the bench. Almost dizzy with fatigue, she climbed into bed and lay atop the quilt, and was asleep the moment her cheek met the pillow.

Downstairs, Cade lifted Bailey's prints from her teacup. He had the connections to have them run quickly and discreetly. If she had a record or had ever worked for the government, he'd have her IDed easily.

He'd check with missing persons, see if anyone matching her description had been reported. That, too, was easy.

The money and the diamond offered another route. The theft of a gem of that size was bound to make news. He needed to verify the facts Bailey had given him on the stone, then do some research.

He needed to check the registration on the gun, too—and check his sources on recent homicides or shootings with a .38.

All those steps would be more effective if done in person. But he didn't want to leave her on her own just yet. She might panic and take off, and he wasn't going to risk losing her.

It was just as possible that she would wake up from

her nap, remember who she was and go back to her own life before he had a chance to save her.

He very much wanted to save her.

While he locked the bag in his library safe, booted up his computer, scribbled his notes, he reminded himself that she might have a husband, six kids, twenty jealous lovers, or a criminal record as long as Pennsylvania Avenue. But he just didn't care.

She was his damsel in distress, and damn it, he was keeping her.

He made his calls, arranged to have the prints messengered over to his contact at the police station. The little favor was going to cost him a bottle of unblended Scotch, but Cade accepted that nothing was free.

"By the way, Mick, you got anything on a jewelry heist? A big one?"

Cade could clearly imagine Detective Mick Marshall pushing through his paperwork, phone cocked at his ear to block out the noise of the bullpen, his tie askew, his wiry red hair sticking up in spikes from a face set in a permanent scowl.

"You got something, Parris?"

"Just a rumor," Cade said easily. "If something big went down, I could use a link to the insurance company. Got to pay the rent, Mick."

"Hell, I don't know why you don't buy the building in the first place, then tear the rattrap down, rich boy."

"I'm eccentric—that's what they call rich boys

who pal around with people like you. So, what do you know?''

"Haven't heard a thing."

"Okay. I've got a Smith and Wesson .38 special." Cade rattled off the serial number as he turned the gun in his hand. "Run it for me, will you?"

"Two bottles of Scotch, Parris."

"What are friends for? How's Doreen?"

"Sassy as ever. Ever since you brought her over those damn tulips, I haven't heard the end of it. Like I got time to pluck posies before I go home every night. I ought to make it three bottles of Scotch.''

"You find out anything about an important gem going missing, Mick, I'll buy you a case. I'll be talking to you."

Cade hung up the phone and stared malevolently at his computer. Man and machine were simply going to have to come to terms for this next bit of research.

It took him what he estimated was three times as long as it would the average twelve-year-old to insert the CD-ROM, search, and find what he was after.

Amnesia.

Cade drank another cup of coffee and learned more about the human brain than he'd ever wanted to know. For a short, uncomfortable time, he feared Bailey had a tumor. That he might have one, as well. He experienced a deep personal concern for his brain stem, then reconfirmed why he hadn't gone into medicine as his mother hoped.

The human body, with all its tricks and ticking time bombs, was just too scary. He'd much rather face a loaded gun than the capriciousness of his own internal organs.

He finally concluded, with some relief, that it was unlikely Bailey had a tumor. All signs pointed to hysterical amnesia, which could resolve itself within hours of the trauma, or take weeks. Months. Even years.

Which put them, he thought, solidly back at square one. The handy medical CD that had come with his computer indicated that amnesia was a symptom, rather than a disease, and that treatment involved finding and removing the cause.

That was where he came in. It seemed to Cade that a detective was every bit as qualified as a doctor to deal with Bailey's problem.

Turning back to his computer, he laboriously typed up his notes, questions and conclusions to date. Satisfied, he went back upstairs to find her some clothes.

She didn't know if it was a dream or reality—or even if it was her own dream or someone else's reality. But it was familiar, so oddly familiar....

The dark room, the hard slant of the beam of light from the desk lamp. The elephant. How strange—the elephant seemed to be grinning at her, its trunk lifted high for luck, its glinting blue eyes gleaming with secret amusement.

Female laughter—again familiar, and so comforting. Friendly, intimate laughter.

It's got to be Paris, Bailey. We're not going to spend two weeks with you digging in the dirt again.

What you need is romance, passion, sex. What you need is Paris.

A triangle, gold and gleaming. And a room filled with light, bright, blinding light. A man who's not a man, with a face so kind, so wise, so generous, it thrills the soul. And the golden triangle held in his open hands, the offering of it, the power of it stunning, the impact of the rich blue of the stones nestled in each angle almost palpable. And the stones shining and pulsing like heartbeats and seeming to leap into the air like stars, shooting stars that scatter light.

The beauty of them sears the eyes.

And she's holding them in her hands, and her hands are shaking. Anger, such anger swirling inside her, and fear and panic and fury. The stones shoot out from her hands, first one, then two, winging away like jeweled birds. And the third is clutched to her heart by her open, protective hand.

Silver flashing, bolts of silver flashing. And the pounding of booming drums that shake the ground. Blood. Blood everywhere, like a hideous river spilling.

My God, it's wet, so red and wet and demon-dark.

Running, stumbling, heart thudding. It's dark again. The light's gone, the stars are gone. There's a corridor, and her heels echo like the thunder that follows lightning. It's coming after her, hunting her in the dark while the walls close in tighter and tighter.

She can hear the elephant trumpeting, and the lightning flashes closer. She crawls into the cave and hides like an animal, shivering and whimpering like an animal as the lightning streaks by her....

"Come on, sweetheart. Come on, honey. It's just a bad dream."

She clawed her way out of the dark toward the calm, steady voice, burrowed her clammy face into the broad, solid shoulder.

"Blood. So much blood. Hit by lightning. It's coming. It's close."

"No, it's gone now." Cade pressed his lips to her hair, rocked her. When he slipped in to leave her a robe, she'd been crying in her sleep. Now she was clinging to him, trembling, so he shifted her into his lap as if she were a child. "You're safe now. I promise."

"The stars. Three stars." Balanced between dream and reality, she shifted restlessly in his arms. "I've got to go to Paris."

"You did. I'm right here." He tipped her head back to touch his lips to her temple. "Right here," he repeated, waiting for her eyes to clear and focus. "Relax now. I'm right here."

"Don't go." With a quick shudder, she rested her head on his shoulder, just as he'd imagined. The pull on his heart was immediate, and devastating.

He supposed love at first sight was meant to be.

"I won't. I'll take care of you."

That alone was enough to ease her trembling. She relaxed against him, let her eyes close again. "It was just a dream, but it was so confusing, so frightening. I don't understand any of it."

"Tell me."

He listened as she struggled to remember the details, put them in order. "There was so much emotion, huge waves of emotions. Anger, shock, a sense of betrayal and fear. Then terror. Just sheer mindless terror."

"That could explain the amnesia. You're not ready to cope with it, so you shut it off. It's a kind of conversion hysteria."

"Hysteria?" The term made her chin lift. "I'm hysterical?"

"In a manner of speaking." He rubbed his knuckles absently over that lifted chin. "It looks good on you."

In a firm, deliberate movement that made his brow quirk, she pushed his hand from her face. "I don't care for the term."

"I'm using it in a strictly medical sense. You didn't get bopped on the head, right?"

Her eyes were narrowed now. "Not that I recall, but then, I'm hysterical, after all."

"Cute. What I mean is, amnesia can result from a concussion." He twirled her hair around his finger as he spoke, just to feel the texture. "I always thought that was bull or Hollywood stuff, but it says so right in the medical book. One of the other causes is a functional nervous disorder, such as—you'll excuse the term—hysteria."

Her teeth were gritted now. "I am not hysterical, though I'm sure I could be, if you'd care for a demonstration."

"I've had plenty of those. I have sisters. Bailey."
He cupped her face in his hands in such a disarming
gesture, her narrowed eyes widened. "You're in trouble, that's the bottom line. And we're going to fix it."

"By holding me in your lap?"

"That's just a side benefit." When her smile fluttered again and she started to shift away, he tightened
his grip. "I like it. A lot."

She could see more than amusement in his eyes,
something that had her pulse jumping. "I don't think
it's wise for you to flirt with a woman who doesn't
know who she is."

"Maybe not, but it's fun. And it'll give you something else to think about."

She found herself charmed, utterly, by the way his
dimples flickered, the way his mouth quirked at the
corner just enough to make the smile crooked. It
would be a good mouth for a lover, quick, clever, full
of energy. She could imagine too well just how it
would fit against hers.

Perhaps because she couldn't imagine any other,
couldn't remember another taste, another texture. And
because that would make him, somehow, the first to
kiss her, the thrill of anticipation sprinted up her
spine.

He dipped her head back, slowly, his gaze sliding
from her eyes to her lips, then back again. He could
imagine it perfectly, and was all but sure there would
be a swell of music to accompany that first meeting
of lips.

"Want to try it?"

Need, rich and full and shocking, poured through her, jittering nerves, weakening limbs. She was alone with him, this stranger she'd trusted her life to. This man she knew more of than she knew of herself.

"I can't." She put a hand on his chest, surprised that however calm his voice his heart was pounding as rapidly as hers. Because it was, she could be honest. "I'm afraid to."

"In my experience, kissing isn't a scary business, unless we're talking about kissing Grandmother Parris, and that's just plain terrifying."

It made her smile again, and this time, when she shifted, he let her go. "Better not to complicate things any more than they are." With restless hands, she scooped her hair back, looked away from him. "I'd like to take a shower, if that's all right. Clean up a little."

"Sure. I brought you a robe, and some jeans you can roll up. The best I could come up with for a belt that would fit you was some clothesline. It'll hold them up and make a unique fashion statement."

"You're very sweet, Cade."

"That's what they all say." He closed off the little pocket of lust within and rose. "Can you handle being alone for an hour? There're a couple of things I should see to."

"Yes, I'll be fine."

"I need you to promise you won't leave the house, Bailey."

She lifted her hands. "Where would I go?"

He put his hands on her shoulders, waited until her

gaze lifted to his. "Promise me you won't leave the house."

"All right. I promise."

"I won't be long." He walked to the door, paused. "And, Bailey? Think about it."

She caught the gleam in his eyes before he turned that told her he didn't mean the circumstances that had brought her to him. When she walked to the window, watched him get in his car and drive away, she was already thinking about it. About him.

Someone else was thinking about her. Thinking dark, vengeful thoughts. She had slipped through his fingers, and, with her, the prize and the power he most coveted.

He'd already exacted a price for incompetence, but it was hardly enough. She would be found, and when she was, she'd pay a much higher price. Her life, certainly, but that was insignificant.

There would be pain first, and great fear. That would satisfy.

The money he had lost was nothing, almost as insignificant as the life of one foolish woman. But she had what he needed, what was meant to belong to him. And he would take back his own.

There were three. Individually they were priceless, but together their value went beyond the imaginable. Already he had taken steps to recover the two she had foolishly attempted to hide from him.

It would take a little time, naturally, but he would have them back. It was important to be careful, to be cautious, to be certain of the recovery, and that whatever violence was necessary remained distant from him.

But soon two pieces of the triangle would be his, two ancient stars, with all their beauty and light and potency.

He sat in the room he'd had built for his treasures, those acquired, stolen or taken with blood. Jewels and paintings, statuary and precious pelts, gleamed and sparkled in his Aladdin's cave of secrets.

The altarlike stand he'd designed to hold his most coveted possession was empty and waiting.

But soon...

He would have the two, and when he had the third he would be immortal.

And the woman would be dead.

Chapter 3

It was her body in the mirror, Bailey told herself, and she'd better start getting used to it. In the glass, fogged from her shower, her skin looked pale and smooth. Self-consciously she laid a hand against her breast.

Long fingers, short trimmed nails, rather small breasts. Her arms were a little thin, she noted with a frown. Maybe she should start thinking about working out to build them up.

There didn't seem to be any excess flab at the waist or hips, so perhaps she got some exercise. And there was some muscle tone in the thighs.

Her skin was pale, without tan lines.

What was she—about five-four? She wished she were taller. It seemed if a woman was going to begin her life at twenty-something, she ought to be able to pick her body type. Fuller breasts and longer legs would have been nice.

Amused at herself, she turned, twisted her head to study the rear view. And her mouth dropped open. There was a tattoo on her butt.

What in the world was she doing with a tattoo of a—was that a unicorn?—on her rear end? Was she crazy? Body decoration was one thing, but on that particular part of the anatomy it meant that she had exposed that particular part of the anatomy to some needle-wielding stranger.

Did she drink too much?

Faintly embarrassed, she pulled on a towel and quickly left the misty bathroom.

She spent some time adjusting the jeans and shirt Cade had left her to get the best fit. Hung up her suit neatly, smoothed the quilt. Then she heaved a sigh and tunneled her fingers through her damp hair.

Cade had asked her to stay in the house, but he hadn't asked her to stay in her room. She was going to be jittery again, thinking about bags of money, huge blue diamonds, murder and tattoos, if she didn't find a distraction.

She wandered out, realizing she wasn't uncomfortable in the house alone. She supposed it was a reflection of her feelings for Cade. He didn't make her uncomfortable. From almost the first minute, she'd felt as though she could talk to him, depend on him.

And she imagined that was because she hadn't talked to anyone else, and had no one else to depend on.

Nonetheless, he was a kind, considerate man. A smart, logical one, she supposed, or else he wouldn't be a private investigator. He had a wonderful smile, full of fun, and eyes that paid attention. He had strength in his arms and, she thought, in his character.

And dimples that made her fingers itch to trace along them.

His bedroom. She gnawed on her lip as she stood in the doorway. It was rude to pry. She wondered if she were rude, careless with the feelings and privacy of others. But she needed something, anything, to fill all these blank spots. And he had left his door open.

She stepped over the threshold.

It was a wonderfully large room, and full of him. Jeans tossed over a chair, socks on the floor. She caught herself before she could pick them up and look for a hamper. Loose change and a couple of shirt buttons tossed on the dresser. A gorgeous antique chest of drawers that undoubtedly held all sorts of pieces of him.

She didn't tug at the brass handles, but she wanted to.

The bed was big, unmade, and framed by the clean lines of Federal head- and footboards. The rumpled sheets were dark blue, and she didn't quite resist running her fingers over them. They'd probably smell of him—that faintly minty scent.

When she caught herself wondering if he slept naked, heat stung her cheeks and she turned away.

There was a neat brick fireplace and a polished pine mantle. A silly brass cow stood on the hearth and made her smile. There were books messily tucked into a recessed shelf. Bailey studied the titles soberly, wondering which she might have read. He went heavy on mysteries and true crime, but there were familiar names. That made her feel better.

Without thinking, she picked up a used coffee mug and an empty beer bottle and carried them downstairs.

She hadn't paid much attention to the house when they came in. It had all been so foggy, so distorted, in her mind. But now she studied the simple and elegant lines, the long, lovely windows, with their classic trim, the gleaming antiques.

The contrast between the gracious home and the second-rate office struck her, made her frown. She rinsed the mug in the sink, found the recycling bin for the bottle, then took herself on a tour.

It took her less than ten minutes to come to her conclusion. The man was loaded.

The house was full of treasures—museum-quality. Of that she was undeniably sure. She might not have understood the unicorn on her own rear end, but she understood the value of a Federal inlaid cherrywood slant-front desk. She couldn't have said why.

She recognized Waterford vases, Georgian silver. The Limoges china in the dining room display cabinet. And she doubted very much if the Turner landscape was a copy.

She peeked out a window. Well-tended lawn, majestic old trees, roses in full bloom. Why would a man who could live in such a style choose to work in a crumbling building in a stuffy, cramped office?

Then she smiled. It seemed Cade Parris was as much a puzzle as she was herself. And that was a tremendous comfort.

She went back to the kitchen, hoping to make herself useful by making some iced tea or putting something together for lunch. When the phone rang, she jumped like a scalded cat. The answering machine clicked on, and Cade's voice flowed out, calming her again: "You've reached 555-2396. Leave a message. I'll get back to you."

"Cade, this is becoming very irritating." The woman's voice was tight with impatience. "I've left a half a dozen messages at your office this morning, the least you can do is have the courtesy to return my calls. I sincerely doubt you're so busy with what you loosely call your clients to speak to your own mother." There was a sigh, long-suffering and loud. "I know very well you haven't contacted Pamela about arrangements for this evening. You've put me in a very awkward position. I'm leaving for Dodie's for bridge. You can reach me there until four. Don't embarrass me, Cade. By the way, Muffy's very annoyed with you."

There was a decisive click. Bailey found herself clearing her throat. She felt very much as if she'd received that cool, deliberate tongue-lashing herself. And it made her wonder if she had a mother who nagged, who expected obedience. Who was worried about her.

She filled the teakettle, set it on the boil, dug up a

pitcher. She was hunting up tea bags when the phone rang again.

"Well, Cade, this is Muffy. Mother tells me she still hasn't been able to reach you. It's obvious you're avoiding our calls because you don't want to face your own poor behavior. You know very well Camilla's piano recital was last night. The least, the very least, you could have done was put in an appearance and pretended to have some family loyalty. Not that I expected any better from you. I certainly hope you have the decency to call Camilla and apologize. I refuse to speak to you again until you do."

Click.

Bailey blew out a breath, rolled her eyes. Families, she thought, were obviously difficult and complex possessions. Then again, perhaps she had a brother herself and was just as, well...bitchy, as the wasp-tongued Muffy.

She set the tea to steep, then opened the refrigerator. There were eggs, and plenty of them. That made her smile. There was also a deli pack of honey-baked ham, some Swiss, and when she discovered plump beefsteak tomatoes, she decided she was in business.

She worried over the choice of mustard or mayo for a time and whether the tea should be sweetened or unsweetened. Every little detail was like a brick in the rebuilding of herself. As she was carefully slicing tomatoes, she heard the front door slam, and her mood brightened.

But when she started to call out, the words stuck in her throat. What if it wasn't Cade? What if they'd found her? Come for her? Her hand tightened on the hilt of the knife as she edged toward the rear kitchen door. Fear, deep and uncontrollable, had sweat popping out in clammy pearls on her skin. Her heart flipped into her throat.

Running, running away from that sharp, hacking lightning. In the dark, with her own breath screaming in her head. Blood everywhere.

Her fingers tensed on the knob, turned it, as she prepared for flight or fight.

When Cade stepped in, a sob of relief burst out of her. The knife clattered on the floor as she launched herself into his arms. "It's you. It is you."

"Sure it is." He knew he should feel guilty that fear had catapulted her against him, but he was only human. She smelled fabulous. "I told you you're safe here, Bailey."

"I know. I felt safe. But when I heard the door, I panicked for a minute." She clung, wildly grateful to have him with her. Drawing her head back, she stared up at him. "I wanted to run, just run, when I heard the door and thought it could be someone else. I hate being such a coward, and not knowing what I should do. I can't seem...to think."

She trailed off, mesmerized. He was stroking her cheek as she babbled, his eyes intent on hers. Her arms were banded around his waist, all but fused there. The hand that had smoothed through her hair was cupped at the base of her neck now, fingers gently kneading.

He waited, saw the change in her eyes. His lips

curved, just enough to have her heart quiver before he lowered his head and gently touched them to hers.

Oh, lovely... That was her first thought. It was lovely to be held so firmly, to be tasted so tenderly. This was a kiss, this sweet meeting of lips that made the blood hum lazily and the soul sigh. With a quiet murmur, she slid her hands up his back, rose on her toes to meet that patient demand.

When his tongue traced her lips, slipped between them, she shuddered with pleasure. And opened to him as naturally as a rose opens to the sun.

He'd known she would. Somehow he'd known she would be both shy and generous, that the taste of her would be fresh, the scent of her airy. It was impossible that he'd only met her hours before. It seemed the woman he held in his arms had been his forever.

And it was thrilling, hotly arousing, to know his was the first kiss she would remember. That he was the only man in her mind and heart to hold her this way, touch her this way. He was the first to make her tremble, his was the first name she murmured when needs swirled through her.

And when she murmured his name, every other woman he'd ever held vanished. She was the first for him.

He deepened the kiss gradually, aware of how easily he could bruise or frighten. But she came so suddenly alive in his arms, was so wildly responsive, her mouth hungry and hot, her body straining and pulsing against his.

She felt alive, brilliantly alive, aware of every frantic beat of her own heart. Her hands had streaked into his hair and were fisted there now, as if she could pull him inside her. He was filling all those empty places, all those frightening blanks. This was life. This was real. This mattered.

"Easy." He could barely get the word out, wished fervently he didn't feel obliged to. He was trembling as much as she, and he knew that if he didn't pull back, gain some control, he was going to take her exactly where they stood. "Easy," he said again, and pressed her head to his shoulder so that he wouldn't be tempted to devour that ripe, willing mouth.

She vibrated against him, nerves and needs tangling, the echoes of sensations thumping through her system. "I don't know if it's ever been like that. I just don't know."

That brought him back to earth a little too abruptly. She didn't know, he reminded himself. He did. It had never been like that for him. "Don't worry." He pulled away, then rubbed his hands over her shoulders, because they were tense again. "You know that wasn't ordinary, Bailey. That ought to be enough for now."

"But—" She bit her lip when he turned and wrenched open the fridge. "I made—I'm making iced tea."

"I want a beer."

She winced at the brusque tone. "You're angry."

"No." He twisted off the cap, downed three long swallows. "Yes. With myself, a little. I pushed the buttons, after all." He lowered the bottle, studied her.

She was standing with her arms crossed tight at her waist. His jeans bagged at her hips, his shirt drooped at her shoulders. Her feet were bare, her hair was tangled around her shoulders.

She looked absolutely defenseless.

"Let's just get this out, okay?" He leaned back against the counter to keep his distance. "I felt the click the minute you walked into the office. Never happened to me before, just click, there she is. I figured it was because you were a looker, you were in trouble and you'd come looking for me. I've got a thing about people in trouble, especially beautiful women."

He drank again, slower this time, while she watched him soberly, with great attention. "But that's not it, Bailey, or at least not all of it. I want to help you. I want to find out everything about you as much as you do. But I also want to make love with you, slow, really slow, so that every second's like an hour. And when we've finished making love, and you're naked and limp under me, I want to start all over again."

She had her hands crossed over her breasts now, to keep her bucking heart in place. "Oh" was all she could manage.

"And that's what I'm going to do. When you're a little steadier on your feet."

"Oh," she said again. "Well." She cleared her throat. "Cade, I may be a criminal."

"Uh-huh." Calm again, he inspected the sandwich makings on the counter. "So is this lunch?"

Her eyes narrowed. What sort of response was that from a man who'd just told her he wanted to make love with her until she was limp? "I may have stolen a great deal of money, killed people, kidnapped an innocent child."

"Right." He piled some ham on bread. "Yeah, you're a real desperado, sweetheart. Anybody can see that. You've got that calculating killer gleam in the eye." Then, chuckling, he turned to her. "Bailey, for God's sake, look at yourself. You're a polite, tidy woman with a conscience as wide as Kansas. I sincerely doubt you have so much as a parking ticket to your name, or that you've done anything wilder than sing in the shower."

It stung. She couldn't have said why, but the bland and goody-goody description put her back up. "I've got a tattoo on my butt."

He set the rather sloppy sandwich he'd put together down. "Excuse me?"

"I have a tattoo on my butt," she repeated, with a combative gleam in her eye.

"Is that so?" He couldn't wait to see it. "Well, then, I'll have to turn you in. Now, if you tell me you've got something other than your ears pierced, I'll have to get my gun."

"I'm so pleased I could amuse you."

"Sweetheart, you fascinate me." He shifted to block her path before she could storm out. "Temper. That's a good sign. Bailey's not a wimp." She stepped to the right. So did he. "She likes scrambled eggs with dill and paprika, knows how to make iced tea, cuts tomatoes in very precise slices and knows how to tie a shank knot.''

''What?''

''Your belt,'' he said with a careless gesture. ''She was probably a Girl Scout, or she likes to sail. Her voice gets icy when she's annoyed, she has excellent taste in clothes, bites her bottom lip when she's nervous—which I should warn you instills wild lust in me for no sensible reason.''

His dimples winked when she immediately stopped nibbling her lip and cleared her throat. ''She keeps her nails at a practical length,'' he continued. ''And she can kiss a man blind. An interesting woman, our Bailey.''

He gave her hair a friendly tug. ''Now, why don't we sit down, eat lunch, and I'll tell you what else I found out. Do you want mustard or mayo?''

''I don't know.'' Still sulking, she plopped down in a chair.

''I go for mustard myself.'' He brought it to the table, along with the fixings for her sandwich. ''So what is it?''

She swiped mustard on bread. ''What?''

''The tattoo? What is it?''

Embarrassed now, she slapped ham over mustard. ''I hardly see that it's an issue.''

''Come on.'' He grinned, leaning over to tug on her hair again. ''A butterfly? A rosebud? Or are you really a biker chick in disguise, with a skull and crossbones hiding under my jeans?''

''A unicorn,'' she muttered.

He bit the tip of his tongue. "Cute." He watched her cut her sandwich into tidy and precise triangles, but refrained from commenting.

Because she wanted to squirm, she changed the subject. "You were going to tell me what else you've found out."

Since it didn't seem to do his blood pressure any good for him to paint mental images of unicorns, he let her off the hook. "Right. The gun's unregistered. My source hasn't been able to trace it yet. The clip's full."

"The clip?"

"The gun was fully loaded, which means it either hadn't been fired recently, or had been reloaded."

"Hadn't been fired." She closed her eyes, grasped desperately at relief. "I might not have used it at all."

"I'd say it's unlikely you did. Using current observations, I can't picture you owning an unregistered handgun, but if we get lucky and track it down, we may have a clearer picture."

"You've learned so much already."

He would have liked to bask in that warm admiration, but he shrugged and took a hefty bite of his sandwich. "Most of it's negative information. There's been no report of a robbery that involves a gem like the one you've been carrying, or that amount of cash. No kidnapping or hostage situations that the local police are involved in, and no open homicides involving the type of weapon we're dealing with in the last week."

He took another swallow of beer. "No one has reported a woman meeting your description missing in the last week, either.''

"But how can that be?'' She shoved her sandwich aside. "I have the gem, I have the cash. I *am* missing.''

"There are possibilities.'' He kept his eyes on hers. "Maybe someone doesn't want that information out. Bailey, you said you thought the diamond was only part of a whole. And when you were coming out of the nightmare you talked about three stars. Stars. Diamonds. Could be the same thing. Do you think there are three of those rocks?''

"Stars?'' She pressed her fingers to her temple as it started to ache. "Did I talk about stars? I don't remember anything about stars.''

Because it hurt to think about it, she tried to concentrate on the reasonable. "Three gems of that size and quality would be unbelievably rare. As a set, even if the others were inferior in clarity to the one I have, they'd be beyond price. You couldn't begin to assess—'' Her breath began to hitch, to come in gasps as she fought for air. "I can't breathe.''

"Okay.'' He was up, shifting her so that he could lower her head between her knees, rub her back. "That's enough for now. Just relax, don't force it.''

He wondered, as he stroked her back, just what she'd seen that put that kind of blind terror in her eyes.

"I'm sorry,'' she managed. "I want to help.''

"You are. You will.'' He eased her up again, waiting as she pushed her hair back away from her pale cheeks. "Hey, it's only day one, remember?"

"Okay." Because he didn't make her feel ashamed of the weakness, she took a deep, cleansing breath. "When I tried to think, really think about what you were asking, it was like a panic attack, with all this guilt and horror and fear mixed together. My head started to throb, and my heart beat too fast. I couldn't get air."

"Then we'll take it slow. You don't get that panicky when we talk about the stone you have?"

She closed her eyes a moment, cautiously brought its image into her mind. It was so beautiful, so extraordinary. There was concern, and worry, yes. A layer of fear, as well, but it was more focused and somehow less debilitating. "No, it's not the same kind of reaction." She shook her head, opened her eyes. "I don't know why."

"We'll work on that." He scooted her plate back in front of her. "Eat. I'm planning a long evening, and you're going to need fuel."

"What sort of plans?"

"I went by the library on my travels. I've got a stack of books on gems—technical stuff, pictures, books on rare stones, rare jewels, the history of diamonds, you name it."

"We might find it." The possibility cheered her enough to have her nibbling on her sandwich again. "If we could identify the stone, we could trace the owner, and then... Oh, but you can't."

"Can't what?"

"Work tonight. You have to go somewhere with Pamela."

"I do? Hell—" He pressed his fingers to his eyes as he remembered.

"I'm sorry, I forgot to mention it. Your mother called. I was in here, so I heard the message. She's upset that you haven't returned her calls, or contacted Pamela about the arrangements for tonight. She's going to be at Dodie's until four. You can call her there. Also, Muffy's very annoyed with you. She called shortly after your mother and she's very unhappy that you missed Camilla's piano recital. She isn't speaking to you until you apologize."

"I should be so lucky," he muttered, and dropped his hands. "That's a pretty good rundown. Want a job?" When she only smiled, he shook his head and rode on inspiration. "No, I'm serious. You're a hell of a lot more organized than my late, unlamented secretary. I could use some help around the office, and you could use the busywork."

"I don't even know if I can type."

"I know I can't, so you're already a step ahead. You can answer a phone, can't you?"

"Of course, but—"

"You'd be doing me a big favor." Calculating her weaknesses, he pressed his advantage. It was the perfect way to keep her close, keep her busy. "I'd rather not take the time to start advertising and interviewing secretaries right now. If you could help me out, a few hours a day, I'd really appreciate it."

She thought of his office, decided it didn't need a

secretary so much as a bulldozer. Well, perhaps she could be of some use after all. "I'd be glad to help."

"Great. Good. Look, I picked up a few things for you while I was out."

"Things?"

"Clothes and stuff."

She stared as he rose and began to clear the plates. "You bought me clothes?"

"Nothing fancy. I had to guess at the sizes, but I've got a pretty good eye." He caught her worrying her lip again and nearly sighed. "Just a few basics, Bailey. As cute as you look in my clothes, you need your own, and you can't wear one suit day after day."

"No, I suppose I can't," she murmured, touched that he should have thought of it. "Thank you."

"No problem. It's stopped raining. You know what you could use? A little fresh air. Let's take a walk, clear your head."

"I don't have any shoes." She took the plates he'd put on the counter and loaded them into the dishwasher.

"I got you some sneakers. Six and a half?"

With a half laugh, she rewrapped the ham. "You tell me."

"Let's try them on and see."

She slid the tray into the dishwasher, closed the door. "Cade, you really have to call your mother."

His grin flashed. "Uh-uh."

"I told you she's upset with you."

"She's always upset with me. I'm the black sheep."

"Be that as it may." Bailey dampened a dishrag and methodically wiped the counters. "She's your mother, and she's waiting for your call."

"No, she's waiting so she can browbeat me into doing something I don't want to do. And when I don't do it, she'll call Muffy, my evil sister, and they'll have a grand old time ripping apart my character."

"That's no way to speak about your family—and you've hurt Camilla's feelings. I assume she's your niece."

"There are rumors."

"Your sister's child."

"No, Muffy doesn't have children, she has creatures. And Camilla is a whiny, pudgy-faced mutant."

She refused to smile, rinsed out the cloth, hung it neatly over the sink. "That's a deplorable way to speak about your niece. Even if you don't like children."

"I do like children." Enjoying himself now, he leaned on the counter and watched her tidy up. "I'm telling you, Camilla's not human. Now my other sister, Doro, she's got two, and somehow the youngest escaped the Parris curse. He's a great kid, likes baseball and bugs. Doro believes he needs therapy."

The chuckle escaped before she swallowed it. "You're making that up."

"Sweetheart, believe me, nothing I could invent about the Parris clan would come close to the horrible truth. They're selfish, self-important and self-indulgent. Are you going to mop the floor now?"

She managed to close her mouth, which had gaped

at his careless condemnation of his own family. Distracted, she glanced down at the glossy ivory tiles. "Oh, all right. Where—"

"Bailey, I'm kidding." He grabbed her hand and tugged her out of the room just as the phone began to ring. "No," he said, before she could open her mouth. "I'm not answering it."

"That's shameful."

"It's self-preservation. I never agreed to this Pamela connection, and I'm not going to be pressured into it."

"Cade, I don't want you to upset your family and break a date on my account. I'll be fine."

"I said I didn't make the date. My mother did. And now, when I have to face the music, I can use you as an excuse. I'm grateful. So grateful I'm going to knock a full day off your fee. Here." He picked up one of the shopping bags he'd dropped by the front door and pulled out a shoe box. "Your glass slippers. If they fit, you get to go to the ball."

Giving up, she sat on the bottom landing and opened the box. Her brow cocked. "Red sneakers?"

"I liked them. They're sexy."

"Sexy sneakers." And she wondered as she undid the laces how she could be in such an enormous mess and find herself delighted over a silly pair of shoes. They slid on like butter, and for some reason made her want to laugh and weep at the same time. "Perfect fit."

"Told you I had a good eye." He smiled when she evened out the laces precisely, tied them into careful and neat bows. "I was right, very sexy." He reached down to draw her to her feet. "In fact, you make quite a package right now."

"I'm sure I do, when the only thing that fits are my shoes." She started to rise to her toes to kiss his cheek, then quickly changed her mind.

"Chicken," he said.

"Maybe." She held out her hand instead. "I'd really love to take a walk." She stepped through the door he opened, glanced up at him. "So is Pamela pretty?"

He considered, decided the straight truth might be to his advantage. "Gorgeous." He closed the door behind them, slipped an arm around Bailey's waist. "And she wants me."

The cool little hum of Bailey's response brought a satisfied smile to his lips.

Chapter 4

Puzzles fascinated him. Locating pieces, shuffling them around, trying new angles until they slipped into place, was a challenge that had always satisfied him. It was one of the reasons Cade had bucked family tradition and chosen his particular line of work.

There was enough rebel in him that he would have chosen almost any line of work that bucked family tradition, but opening his own investigation agency had the added benefit of allowing him to call his own shots, solve those puzzles and right a few wrongs along the way.

He had very definite opinions on right and wrong. There were good guys and there were bad guys, there was law and there was crime. Still, he wasn't naive or simplistic enough not to understand and appreciate the shades of gray. In fact, he often visited gray areas, appreciated them. But there were certain lines that didn't get crossed.

He also had a logical mind that occasionally took recreational detours into the fanciful.

Most of all, he just loved figuring things out.

He'd spent a good deal of time at the library after he left Bailey that morning, scanning reams of microfiche, hunting for any snippet of news on a stolen blue diamond. He hadn't had the heart to point out to her that they had no idea where she came from. She might have traveled to D.C. from anywhere over the past few days.

The fact that she, the diamond and the cash were here now didn't mean that was where they had started out. Neither of them had any idea just how long her memory had been blank.

He'd studied up further on amnesia, but he hadn't found anything particularly helpful. As far as he could tell, anything could trigger her memory, or it could remain wiped clean, with her new life beginning shortly before she'd walked into his.

He had no doubt she'd been through or witnessed something traumatic. And though it might be considered one of those detours into the fanciful he was sometimes accused of having, he was certain she was innocent of any wrongdoing.

How could a woman with eyes like hers have done anything criminal?

Whatever the answers were, he was dead set on one thing—he meant to protect her. He was even ready to accept the simple fact that he'd fallen for her the moment he saw her. Whoever and whatever Bailey was, she was the woman he'd been waiting for.

So he not only meant to protect her—he meant to keep her.

He'd chosen his first wife for all the logical and traditional reasons. Or, he mused, he'd been fingered—calculatingly—by his in-laws, and also by his own family. And that soulless merger had been a disaster in its very reasonableness.

Since the divorce—which had ruffled everyone's feathers except those of the two people most involved—he'd dodged and evaded commitment with a master's consummate skill at avoidance.

He believed the reason for all that was sitting cross-legged on the rug beside him, peering myopically at a book on gemstones.

"Bailey, you need glasses."

"Hmm?" She had all but pressed her nose into the page.

"It's just a wild guess, but I'd say you usually wear reading glasses. If your face gets any closer to that book, you're going to be in it."

"Oh." She blinked, rubbed her eyes. "It's just that the print's awfully small."

"Nope. Don't worry, we'll take care of that tomorrow. We've been at this a couple hours. Want a glass of wine?"

"I suppose." Chewing on her bottom lip, she struggled to bring the text into focus. "The Star of Africa is the largest known cut diamond in existence at 530.2 carats."

"Sounds like a whopper," Cade commented as he chose the bottle of Sancerre he'd been saving for the right occasion.

"It's set in the British royal scepter. It's too big, and it's not a blue diamond. So far I haven't found anything that matches our stone. I wish I had a refractometer."

"A what?"

"A refractometer," she repeated, pushing at her hair. "It's an instrument that measures the characteristic property of a stone. The refractive index." Her hand froze as he watched her. "How do I know that?"

Carrying two glasses, he settled on the floor beside her again. "What's the refractive index?"

"It's the relative ability to refract light. Diamonds are singly refracting. Cade, I don't understand how I know that."

"How do you know it's not a sapphire?" He picked up the stone from where it sat like a paperweight on his notes. "It sure looks like one to me."

"Sapphires are doubly refracting." She shuddered. "I'm a jewel thief. That must be how I know."

"Or you're a jeweler, a gem expert, or a really rich babe who likes to play with baubles." He handed her a glass. "Don't jump to conclusions, Bailey. That's how you miss details."

"Okay." But she had an image of herself dressed all in black, climbing in second-story windows. She drank deeply. "I just wish I could understand why I remember certain things. Refractometers, *The Maltese Falcon*—''

''*The Maltese Falcon?*''

''The movie—Bogart, Mary Astor. You had the book in your room, and the movie jumped right into my head. And roses, I know what they smell like, but I don't know my favorite perfume. I know what a unicorn is, but I don't know why I've got a tattoo of one.''

''It's a unicorn.'' His lips curved up, dimples flashing. ''Symbol of innocence.''

She shrugged that off and drank down the rest of her wine quickly. Cade merely passed her his own glass and got up to refill. ''And there was this tune playing around in my head while I was in the shower. I don't know what it is, but I couldn't get rid of it.'' She sipped again, frowned in concentration, then began to hum.

''Beethoven's 'Ode to Joy,''' he told her. ''Beethoven, Bogart and a mythical beast. You continue to fascinate me, Bailey.''

''And what kind of name is Bailey?'' she demanded, gesturing expansively with her glass. ''Is it my last name or my first? Who would stick a child with a first name like Bailey? I'd rather be Camilla.''

He grinned again, wondered if he should take the wine out of her reach. ''No, you wouldn't. Take my word for it.''

She blew the hair out of her eyes and pouted.

''Tell me about diamonds.''

"They're a girl's best friend." She chuckled, then beamed at him. "Did I make that up?"

"No, honey, you didn't." Gently, he took the half-empty glass from her, set it aside. Mental note, he thought—Bailey's a one-drink wonder. "Tell me what you know about diamonds."

"They sparkle and shine. They look cold, even feel cold to the touch. That's how you can easily identify glass trying to pass. Glass is warm, diamonds are cold. That's because they're excellent heat conductors. Cold fire."

She lay on her back, stretching like a cat, and had saliva pooling in his mouth. She closed her eyes.

"It's the hardest substance known, with a value of ten on Mohs' hardness scale. All good gem diamonds are white diamonds. A yellowish or brown tinge is considered an imperfection."

My, oh, my, she thought, and sighed, feeling her head spin. "Blue, green and red diamonds are very rare and highly prized. The color's caused by the presence of minor elements other than pure carbon."

"Good." He studied her face, the curved lips, closed eyes. She might have been talking of a lover. "Keep going."

"In specific gravity, diamonds range between 3.15 and 3.53, but the value for pure crystals is almost always 3.52. You need brilliancy and fire," she murmured, stretching lazily again.

Despite his good intentions, his gaze shifted, and he watched her small, firm breasts press against the material of his shirt. "Yeah, I bet."

"Uncut diamonds have a greasy luster, but when cut, oh, they shine." She rolled over on her stomach, bent her legs into the air and crossed her ankles. "This is characterized technically as adamantine. The name *diamond* is derived from the Greek word *adamas,* meaning 'invincible.' There's such beauty in strength."

She opened her eyes again, and they were heavy and clouded. She shifted, swinging her legs around until she was sitting, all but in his lap. "You're awfully strong, Cade. And so pretty. When you kissed me, it felt like you could gobble me right up, and I couldn't do a thing about it." She sighed, wiggled a bit to get comfortable, then confided, "I really liked it."

"Oh, boy." He felt the blood begin its slow, leisurely journey from head to loins and cautiously covered both the hands she had laid on his chest. "Better switch to coffee."

"You want to kiss me again."

"About as much as I'd like to take the next breath." That mouth of hers was ripe and willing and close. Her eyes were dreamy and dark.

And she was plowed.

"Let's just hold off on that."

Gently he started to ease her back, but she was busily crawling the rest of the way into his lap. In a smooth, agile movement, she wriggled down and hooked her legs around his waist.

"I don't think— Listen—" For a damsel in distress, she had some pretty clever moves. He managed to catch her industrious hands again before she pulled his shirt off. "Cut that out. I mean it."

He did mean it, he realized, and accepted the new fact that he was insane.

"Do you think I'd be good in bed?" The question nearly had his eyes crossing and his tongue tied in knots. She, meanwhile, simply sighed, settled her head on his shoulder and murmured, "I hope I'm not frigid."

"I don't think there's much chance of that." Cade's blood pressure spiked while she nibbled delicately on his earlobe. Her hands snuck under his shirt and up his back with a light scraping of nails.

"You taste so good," she noted approvingly, her lips moving down his throat. "I'm awfully hot. Are you hot?"

With an oath, he turned his head, captured her mouth and devoured.

She was ripe with flavors, pulsing with heat. He let himself sink into her, drown in that hot, delicious mouth, while the humming purrs that rippled from her throat pounded through his system like diamonds cased in velvet.

She was pliant, almost fluid, in surrender. When she dipped her head back, offering her throat, no saint in heaven could have resisted it. He scraped his teeth over that smooth white column, listened to her moan, felt her move sinuously against him in invitation.

He could have taken her, simply laid her back on the books and papers and buried himself in her. He could almost feel that glorious slippery friction, the rhythm that would be theirs and only theirs.

And as much as he knew it would be right, it would be perfect, he knew it couldn't be either, not then, not there.

"I've never wanted anyone as much as I want you." He plunged his hand into her hair, turning her head until their eyes met. "Damn it, focus for a minute. Look at me."

She couldn't see anything else. She didn't want anything else. Her body felt light as air, her mind empty of everything but him. "Kiss me again, Cade. It's like a miracle when you do."

Praying for strength, he lowered his brow to hers until he could steady his breathing. "Next time I kiss you, you're going to know just what's going on." He rose and lifted her into his arms.

"My head's spinning." Giggling, she let it fall back on his supporting arm.

"Whose isn't?" With what he considered really heroic control, he laid her on the couch. "Take a nap."

"'Kay." Obediently, she closed her eyes. "You'll stay here. I feel safe when you're here."

"Yeah, I'll be here." He dragged his hands through his hair and watched her drift off. They were going to laugh at this someday, he thought. Maybe when they had grandchildren.

Leaving her sleeping, he went back to work.

…She was digging in the dirt. The sun was a torch in a sapphire sky. The surrounding land was rocky

and baked into muted shades of browns and reds and
lavenders. Strong and pungent was the scent of sage
from the pale green shrubs struggling out of cracks
and crevices in the earth. With spade and hammer,
she went about her work happily.

Under the narrow shade of a boulder, two women
sat watching her. Her sense of contentment was
strong, and stronger yet when she looked over and
smiled at them.

One had a short cap of hair that glowed like copper
and a sharp, foxy face. And, though her eyes were
shielded by dark wraparound sunglasses, Bailey knew
they were a deep, deep green.

The other had ebony hair, though it was tucked up
now under a wide-brimmed straw hat with silly red
flowers around the crown. Loose, the hair would fall
past her shoulder blades, thick and wavy to the waist.
It suited the magic of her face, the creamy complex-
ion and impossibly blue eyes.

Bailey felt a wave of love just from looking at
them, a bond of trust and a sense of shared lives.
Their voices were like music, a distant song of which
she could only catch snatches.

Could go for a cold beer.

A cold anything.

How long do you think she'll keep at it?

*For the rest of our lives. Paris next summer. Defi-
nitely.*

Get her away from rocks long enough.

And the creeps.

Definitely.

It made her smile that they were talking about her, cared enough to talk about her. She'd go to Paris with them. But for now, she chinked away at an interesting formation, hoping to find something worthwhile, something she could take back and study, then fashion into something pretty for her friends.

It took patience, and a good eye. Whatever she found today, she'd share with them.

Then, suddenly, the blue stones all but tumbled into her hand. Three perfect blue diamonds of spectacular size and luster. And it was with pleasure, rather than shock, that she examined them, turned them in her palms, then felt the jolt of power sing through her body.

The storm rolled in fast and mean, blocking the flaming sun, dark, grasping shadows shooting out and covering the landscape. Now there was panic, a great need to hurry. Hurry. Hurry. A stone for each of them, before it was too late. Before the lightning struck.

But it was already too late. Lightning stabbed the skin, sharp as a knife, and she was running, running blindly. Alone and terrified, with the walls closing in and the lightning stabbing at her heels....

She awoke with her breath heaving, shooting straight up on the sofa. What had she done? Dear God, what had she done? Rocking herself, her hands pressed to her mouth, Bailey waited for the shudders to pass.

The room was quiet. There was no thunder, no lightning, no storm chasing her. And she wasn't alone. Across the room, under the slant of light from a globe lamp, Cade dozed in a chair. He had a book open on his lap.

It calmed her just to see him there, papers scattered at his feet, a mug on the table beside him. His legs were stretched out, crossed comfortably at the ankles.

Even in sleep, he looked strong, dependable. He hadn't left her alone. She had to block an urge to go over, crawl into his lap and slide back to sleep cuddled with him. He pulled her, tugged at her emotions so strongly. It didn't seem to matter that she'd known him less than twenty-four hours. After all, she'd hardly known herself much longer.

Pushing at her hair, she glanced at her watch. It was just after three a.m., a vulnerable time. Stretching out again, she pillowed her head on her hands and watched him. Her memory of the evening was clear enough, no breaks, no jumps. She knew she'd thrown herself at him, and it both embarrassed and amazed her.

He'd been right to stop before matters got out of hand. She knew he was right.

But, oh, she wished he'd just taken her, there on the floor. Taken her before she had all this time to think about the right and wrong of it, the consequences.

Some of this emptiness within her would be filled now, some of those undefinable needs met.

Sighing, she rolled to her back and stared up at the ceiling. But he'd been right to stop. She had to think.

She closed her eyes, not to seek sleep but to welcome memory. Who were the women she'd dreamed

of? And where were they now? Despite herself she
drifted off.

Cade woke the next morning stiff as a board. Bones
popped as he stretched. He rubbed his hands over his
face, and his palms made scratching sounds against
the stubble. The moment his eyes cleared, he looked
across the room. The couch was empty.

He might have thought he'd dreamed her, if not for
the books and papers heaped all over the floor. The
whole thing seemed like a dream—the beautiful, troubled woman with no past, walking into his life and
his heart at the same time. In the morning light, he
wondered how much he'd romanticized it, this connection he felt with her. Love at first sight was a
romantic notion under the best of circumstances.

And these were hardly the best.

She didn't need him mooning over her, he reminded himself. She needed his mind to be clear.
Daydreaming about the way she'd wrapped herself
around him and asked him to make love with her
simply wasn't conducive to logical thinking.

He needed coffee.

He rose and trying to roll the crick out of his neck,
headed for the kitchen.

And there she was, pretty as a picture and neat as
a pin. Her hair was smooth, brushed to a golden luster
and pulled back with a simple rubber band. She was
wearing the navy-and-white striped slacks he'd
bought her, with a white camp shirt tucked into the
waist. With one hand resting on the counter, the other

holding a steaming mug, she was staring out the window at his backyard where a rope hammock hung between twin maples and roses bloomed.

"You're an early riser."

Her hand shook in startled reaction to his voice, and then she turned, worked up a smile. Her heart continued to thud just a little too fast when she saw him, rumpled from sleep. "I made coffee. I hope you don't mind."

"Sweetheart, I owe you my life." He said in heartfelt tones as he reached for a mug.

"It seems I know how to make it. Apparently some things just come naturally. I didn't even have to think about it. It's a little strong. I must like it strong."

He was already downing it, reveling in the way it seared his mouth and jolted his system. "Perfect."

"Good. I didn't know if I should wake you. I wasn't sure what time you leave for your office, or how much time you'd need."

"It's Saturday, and the long holiday weekend."

"Holiday?"

"Fourth of July." While the caffeine pumped through his system, he topped off his mug. "Fireworks, potato salad, marching bands."

"Oh." She had a flash of a little girl sitting on a woman's lap as lights exploded in the night sky. "Of course. You'll be taking the weekend off. You must have plans."

"Yeah, I got plans. I plan for us to toddle into the office about midmorning. I can show you the ropes. Won't be able to do much legwork today, with everything shut down, but we can start putting things in order.''

"I don't want you to give up your weekend. I'd be happy to go in and straighten up your office, and you could—"

"Bailey. I'm in this with you."

She set her mug down, linked her hands. "Why?"

"Because it feels right to me. The way I see it, what you can't figure out in your head, you do on instinct." Those sea-mist eyes roamed over her face, then met hers. "I like to think there's a reason you picked me. For both of us."

"I'm surprised you can say that, after the way I acted last evening. For all we know, I go out cruising bars every night and pick up strange men."

He chuckled into his mug. Better to laugh, he'd decided, than to groan. "Bailey, the way a single glass of wine affects you, I doubt you spent much time in bars. I've never seen anyone get bombed quite that fast."

"I don't think that's anything to be proud of." Her voice had turned stiff and cool, and it made him want to grin again.

"It's nothing to be ashamed of either. And you didn't pick a strange man, you picked me." The amusement in his eyes flicked off. "We both know it was personal, with or without the alcohol."

"Then why didn't you…take advantage?"

"Because that's just what it would have been. I don't mind having the advantage, but I'm not interested in taking it. Want breakfast?"

She shook her head, waited until he'd gotten out a box of cereal and a bowl. "I appreciate your restraint."

"Do you?"

"Not entirely."

"Good." He felt the muscles of his ego expand and flex as he got milk out of the refrigerator. He poured it on, then added enough sugar to have Bailey's eyes widening.

"That can't be healthy."

"I live for risk." He ate standing up. "Later I thought we'd drive downtown, walk around with the tourists. You may see something that jogs your memory."

"All right." She hesitated, then took a chair. "I don't know anything about your work, really, your usual clientele. But it seems to me you're taking all of this completely in stride."

"I love a mystery." Then he shrugged and shoveled in more cereal. "You're my first amnesia case, if that's what you mean. My usual is insurance fraud and domestic work. It has its moments."

"Have you been an investigator very long?"

"Four years. Five, if you count the year I trained as an operative with Guardian. They're a big security firm here in D.C. Real suit-and-tie stuff. I like working on my own better."

"Have you ever...had to shoot at someone?"

"No. Too bad, really, because I'm a damn good shot." He caught her gnawing her lip and shook his head. "Relax, Bailey. Cops and P.I.s catch the bad guys all the time without drawing their weapon. I've taken a few punches, given a few, but mostly it's just legwork, repetition and making calls. Your problem's just another puzzle. It's just a matter of finding all the pieces and fitting them together.''

She hoped he was right, hoped it could be just that simple, that ordinary, that logical. "I had another dream. There were two women. I knew them, I'm sure of it.'' When he pulled out a chair and sat across from her, she told him what she remembered.

"It sounds like you were in the desert,'' he said when she fell silent. "Arizona, maybe New Mexico.''

"I don't know. But I wasn't afraid. I was happy, really happy. Until the storm came.''

"There were three stones, you're sure of that?''

"Yes, almost identical, but not quite. I had them, and they were so beautiful, so extraordinary. But I couldn't keep them together. That was very important.'' She sighed. "I don't know how much was real and how much was jumbled and symbolic, the way dreams are.''

"If one stone's real, there may be two more.'' He took her hand. "If one woman's real, there may be two more. We just have to find them.''

It was after ten when they walked into his office. The cramped and dingy work space struck her as more than odd now that she'd seen how he lived. But she listened carefully as he tried to explain how to work the computer to type up his notes, how he thought the filing should be done, how to handle the phone and intercom systems.

When he left her alone to close himself in his office, Bailey surveyed the area. The philodendron lay on its side, spilling dirt. There was broken glass, sticky splotches from old coffee, and enough dust to shovel.

Typing would just have to wait, she decided. No one could possibly concentrate in such a mess.

From behind his desk, Cade used the phone to do his initial legwork. He tracked down his travel agent and, on the pretext of planning a vacation, asked her to locate any desert area where rockhounding was permitted. He told her he was exploring a new hobby.

From his research the night before, he'd learned quite a bit about the hobby of unearthing crystals and gems. The way Bailey had described her dream, he was certain that was just what she'd been up to.

Maybe she was from out west, or maybe she'd just visited there. Either way, it was another road to explore.

He considered calling in a gem expert to examine the diamond. But on the off chance that Bailey had indeed come into its possession by illegal means, he didn't want to risk it.

He took the photographs he'd snapped the night before of the diamond and spread them out on his desk. Just how much would a gemologist be able to tell from pictures? he wondered.

It might be worth a try. Tuesday, when businesses

were open again, he mused, he might take that road, as well.

But he had a couple of other ideas to pursue.

There was another road, an important one, that had to be traveled first. He picked up the phone again, began making calls. He pinned Detective Mick Marshall down at home.

"Damn it, Cade, it's Saturday. I've got twenty starving people outside and burgers burning on the grill."

"You're having a party and didn't invite me? I'm crushed."

"I don't have play cops at my barbecues."

"Now you've really hurt my feelings. Did you earn that Scotch?"

"No match on those prints you sent me. Nothing popped."

Cade felt twin tugs of relief and frustration. "Okay. Still no word on a missing rock?"

"Maybe if you told me what kind of rock."

"A big glittery one. You'd know if it had been reported."

"Nothing's been reported, and I think the rocks are in your head, Parris. Now unless you're going to share, I've got hungry mouths to feed."

"I'll get back to you on it. And the Scotch."

He hung up, and spent some time thinking.

Lightning kept coming up in Bailey's dreams. There'd been thunderstorms the night before she came into his office. It could be as simple as that—

one of the last things she remembered was thunder and lightning. Maybe she had a phobia about storms.

She talked about the dark, too. There'd been some power outages downtown that night. He'd already checked on that. Maybe the dark was literal, rather than symbolic.

He guessed she'd been inside. She hadn't spoken of rain, of getting wet. Inside a house? An office building? If whatever had happened to her had happened the night before she came to him, then it almost certainly had to have occurred in the D.C. area.

But no gem had been reported missing.

Three kept cropping up in her dreams, as well. Three stones. Three stars. Three women. A triangle.

Symbolic or real?

He began to take notes again, using two columns. In one he listed her dream memories as literal memories, in the other he explored the symbolism.

And the longer he worked, the more he leaned toward the notion that it was a combination of both.

He made one last call, and prepared to grovel. His sister Muffy had married into one of the oldest and most prestigious family businesses in the East. Westlake Jewelers.

When Cade stepped back into the outer office, his ears were still ringing and his nerves were shot. Those were the usual results of a conversation with his sister. But since he'd wangled what he wanted, he tried to take things in stride.

The shock of walking into a clean, ordered room and seeing Bailey efficiently rattling the keyboard on the computer went a long way toward brightening his mood.

"You're a goddess." He grabbed her hand, kissed it lavishly. "A worker of miracles."

"This place was filthy. Disgusting."

"Yeah, it probably was."

Her brows lowered. "There was food molding in the file cabinets."

"I don't doubt it. You know how to work a computer."

She frowned at the screen. "Apparently. It was like making the coffee this morning. No thought."

"If you know how to work it, you know how to turn it off. Let's go downtown. I'll buy you an ice cream cone."

"I've just gotten started."

"It can wait." He reached down to flick the switch, and she slapped his hand away.

"No. I haven't saved it." Muttering under her breath, she hit a series of keys with such panache, his heart swelled in admiration. "I'll need several more hours to put things in order around here."

"We'll come back. We've got a couple hours to kick around, then we've got some serious work to do."

"What kind of work?" she demanded as he hauled her to her feet.

"I've got you access to a refractometer." He pulled her out the door. "What kind of ice cream do you want?"

Chapter 5

"Your brother-in-law owns Westlake Jewelers?"

"Not personally. It's a family thing."

"A family thing." Bailey's head was still spinning. Somehow she'd gone from cleaning molded sandwiches out of filing cabinets to eating strawberry ice cream on the steps of the Lincoln Memorial. That was confusing enough, but the way Cade had whipped through traffic, zipping around circles and through yellow lights, had left her dizzy and disoriented.

"Yep." He attacked his two scoops of rocky road. Since she'd stated no preference, he'd gotten her strawberry. He considered it a girl flavor. "They have branches all over the country, but the flagship store's here. Muffy met Ronald at a charity tennis tournament when she beaned him with a lob. Very romantic."

"I see." Or she was trying to. "And he agreed to let us use the equipment?"

"Muffy agreed. Ronald goes along with whatever Muffy wants."

Bailey licked her dripping cone, watched the tourists—the families, the children—clamber up and down the steps. "I thought she was angry with you."

"I talked her out of it. Well, I bribed her. Camilla also takes ballet. There's a recital next month. So I'll go watch Camilla twirl around in a tutu, which, believe me, is not a pretty sight."

Bailey choked back a chuckle. "You're so mean."

"Hey, I've seen Camilla in a tutu, you haven't. Take my word, I'm being generous." He liked seeing her smile, just strolling along with him eating strawberry ice cream and smiling. "Then there's Chip. That's Muffy's other mutant. He plays the piccolo."

"I'm sure you're making this up."

"I couldn't make it up, my imagination has limits. In a couple of weeks I have to sit front and center and listen to Chip and his piccolo at a band concert." He shuddered. "I'm buying earplugs. Let's sit down."

They settled on the smooth steps beneath the wise and melancholy president. There was a faint breeze that helped stir the close summer air. But it could do little about the moist heat that bounced, hard as damp bricks, up from the sidewalks. Bailey could see waves of it shimmer, like desert mirages, in the air.

There was something oddly familiar about all of it, the crowds of people passing, pushing strollers, clicking cameras, the mix of voices and accents, the smells of sweat, humanity and exhaust, flowers blooming in their plots, vendors hawking their wares.

"I must have been here before," she murmured. "But it's just out of sync. Like someone else's dream."

"It's going to come back to you." He tucked a stray strand of hair behind her ear. "Pieces already are. You know how to make coffee, use a computer, and you can organize an office."

"Maybe I'm a secretary."

He didn't think so. The way she rattled off information on diamonds the evening before had given him a different idea. But he wanted to weigh it awhile before sharing it. "If you are, I'll double your salary if you work for me." Keeping it light, he rose and offered her a hand. "We've got some shopping to do."

"We do?"

"You need reading glasses. Let's hit the stores."

It was another experience, the sprawling shopping center packed with people looking for bargains. The holiday sale was in full swing. Despite the heat, winter coats were displayed and discounted twenty percent, and fall fashions crowded out the picked over remains of summer wear.

Cade deposited her at a store that promised glasses within an hour and filled out the necessary forms himself while she browsed the walls of frames available.

There was a quick, warm glow that spread inside

him when he listed her name as Bailey Parris and
wrote his own address. It looked right to him, felt
right. And when she was led into the back for the
exam—free with the purchase of frames—he gave her
a kiss on the cheek.

In less than two hours, she was back in his car,
examining her pretty little wire-framed glasses, and
the contents of a loaded shopping bag.

"How did you have time to buy all of this?" With
a purely feminine flutter, she smoothed a hand over
the smooth leather of a bone shoulder-strap envelope
bag.

"It's all a matter of stategy and planning, knowing
what you want and not being distracted."

Bailey peeked in a bag from a lingerie store and
saw rich black silk. Gingerly she pulled the material
out. There wasn't a great deal of it, she mused.

"You've got to sleep in something," Cade told her.
"It was on sale. They were practically giving it
away."

She might not have known who she was, but she
was pretty sure she knew sleepwear from seduce-me
wear. She tucked the silk back in the bag. Digging
deeper, she discovered a bag of crystals. "Oh, they're
lovely."

"They had one of those nature stores. So I picked
up some rocks." He braked at a stop sign and shifted
so that he could watch her. "Picked out a few that
appealed to me. The smooth ones are... What do you
call it?"

"Tumbling stones," she murmured, stroking them

gently with a fingertip. "Carnelian, citrine, sodalite, jasper." Flushed with pleasure, she unwrapped tissue. "Tourmaline, watermelon tourmaline—see the pinks and the greens?—and this is a lovely column of fluorite. It's one of my favorites. I…" She trailed off, pressed a hand to her temple.

He reached in himself, took out a stone at random. "What's this?"

"Alexandrite. It's a chrysoberyl, a transparent stone. Its color changes with the light. See it's blue-green now, in daylight, but in incandescent light it would be mauve or violet." She swallowed hard because the knowledge was there, just there in her mind. "It's a multipurpose stone, but scarce and expensive. It was named for Czar Alexander I."

"Okay, relax, take a deep breath." He made the turn, headed down the tree-lined street. "You know your stones, Bailey."

"Apparently I do."

"And they give you a lot of pleasure." Her face had lit up, simply glowed, when she studied his choices.

"It scares me. The more the information crowded inside my head, the more it scared me."

He pulled into his driveway, turned to her. "Are you up to doing the rest of this today?"

She could say no, she realized. He would take her inside then, inside his house, where she'd be safe. She could go up to the pretty bedroom, close herself in. She wouldn't have to face anything but her own cowardice.

"I want to be. I will be," she added, and let out a long breath. "I have to be."

"Okay." Reaching over, he gave her hand a quick squeeze. "Just sit here. I'll get the diamond."

Westlake Jewelers was housed in a magnificent old building with granite columns and long windows draped in satin. It was not the place for bargains. The only sign was a discreet and elegant brass plate beside the arched front entrance.

Cade drove around the back.

"They're getting ready to close for the day," he explained. "If I know Muffy, she'll have Ronald here waiting. He may not be too thrilled with me, so... Yeah, there's his car." Cade shot his own into a space beside a sedate gray Mercedes sedan. "You just play along with me, all right?"

"Play along?" She wrinkled her brow as he dumped stones into her new handbag. "What do you mean?"

"I had to spin a little story to talk her into this." Reaching over, he opened Bailey's door. "Just go along."

She got out, walked with him to the rear entrance. "It might help if I knew what I was going along with."

"Don't worry." He rang the buzzer. "I'll handle it."

She shifted her now heavy bag on her shoulder. "If you've lied to your family, I think I ought to—" She broke off when the heavy steel door opened.

"Cade." Ronald Westlake nodded curtly. Cade had been right, Bailey thought instantly. This was not a happy man. He was average height, trim and well presented, in a dark blue suit with a muted striped tie so ruthlessly knotted she wondered how he could draw breath. His face was tanned, his carefully styled hair dark and discreetly threaded with glinting gray.

Dignity emanated from him like light.

"Ronald, good to see you," Cade said cheerily, and as if Ronald's greeting had been filled with warmth, he pumped his hand enthusiastically. "How's the golf game? Muffy tells me you've been shaving that handicap."

As he spoke, Cade eased himself inside, much, Bailey thought, like a salesman with his foot propped in a door. Ronald continued to frown and back up.

"This is Bailey. Muffy might have told you a little about her." In a proprietary move, Cade wrapped his arm around Bailey's shoulder and pulled her to his side.

"Yes, how do you do?"

"I've been keeping her to myself," Cade added before Bailey could speak. "I guess you can see why." Smoothly Cade tipped Bailey's face up to his and kissed her. "I appreciate you letting us play with your equipment. Bailey's thrilled. Sort of a busman's holiday for her, showing me how she works with stones." He shook her purse so that the stones inside rattled.

"You've never shown any interest in gems before," Ronald pointed out.

"I didn't know Bailey before," Cade said easily. "Now, I'm fascinated. And now that I've talked her into staying in the States, she's going to have to think about setting up her own little boutique. Right, sweetheart?"

"I—"

"England's loss is our gain," he continued. "And if one of the royals wants another bauble, they'll have to come here. I'm not letting you get away." He kissed her again, deeply, while Ronald stood huffing and tugging at his tie.

"Cade tells me you've been designing jewelry for some time. It's quite an endorsement, having the royal family select your work."

"It's sort of keeping it in the family, too," Cade said with a wink. "With Bailey's mama being one of Di's cousins. Was that third or fourth cousin, honey? Oh, well, what's the difference?"

"Third," Bailey said, amazed at herself not only for answering, but also for infusing her voice with the faintest of upper-class British accents. "They're not terribly close. Cade's making too much of it. It's simply that a few years ago a lapel pin I'd fashioned caught the eye of the Princess of Wales. She's quite a keen shopper, you know."

"Yes, yes, indeed." The tony accent had a sizable effect on a man with Ronald's social requirements. His smile spread, his voice warmed. "I'm delighted you could stop by. I do wish I could stay, show you around."

"We don't want to keep you." Cade was already

thumping Ronald on the back. "Muffy told me you're entertaining."

"It's terribly presumptuous of Cade to interrupt your holiday. I would so love a tour another time."

"Of course, anytime, anytime at all. And you must try to drop by the house later this evening." Pumped up at the thought of entertaining even such a loose connection with royalty, Ronald began to usher them toward the jeweler's work area. "We're very select in our equipment, as well as our stones. The Westlake reputation has been unimpeachable for generations."

"Ah, yes." Her heart began to thud as she studied the equipment in the glass-walled room, the worktables, the saws, the scales. "Quite top-of-the-line."

"We pride ourselves on offering our clientele only the best. We often cut and shape our own gems here, and employ our own lapidaries."

Bailey's hand shook lightly as she passed it over a wheel. A lap, she thought, used to shape the stone. She could see just how it was done—the stone cemented to the end of a wooden stick, a dop, held against the revolving lap wheel with the aid of a supporting block adjacent to the wheel.

She knew, could hear the sounds of it. Feel the vibrations.

"I enjoy lap work," Bailey said faintly. "The precision of it."

"I'm afraid I only admire the craftsmen and artists. That's a stunning ring. May I?" Ronald took her left hand, examined the trio of stones arranged in a gentle curve and set in etched gold. "Lovely. Your design?"

"Yes." It seemed the best answer. "I particularly enjoy working with colored stones."

"You must see our stock sometime soon." Ronald glanced at his watch, clucked his tongue. "I'm running quite late. The security guard will let you back out when you're done. Please take all the time you want. I'm afraid the showroom itself is locked, time-locked, and you'll need the guard to open the rear door, as it engages from inside and out." He sent Bailey a professional-to-professional smile. "You'd understand how important security is in the business."

"Of course. Thank you so much for your time, Mr. Westlake."

Ronald took Bailey's offered hand. "Ronald, please. And it's my pleasure. You mustn't let Cade be so selfish of you. Muffy is very much looking forward to meeting her future sister-in-law. Be sure to drop by later."

Bailey made a strangled sound, easily covered by Cade's quick chatter as he all but shoved Ronald out of the work area.

"Sister-in-law?" Bailey managed.

"I had to tell them something." All innocence, Cade spread his hands. "They've been campaigning to get me married off again since the ink was dry on my divorce decree. And you being royalty, so to speak, puts you several societal steps up from the women they've been pushing on me."

"Poor Cade. Having women shoved at him right and left."

"I've suffered." Because there were dangerous glints in her eyes, he tried his best smile. "You have no idea how I've suffered. Hold me."

She slapped his hand away. "Is this all a big joke to you?"

"No, but that part of it was fun." He figured his hands would be safer in his pockets. "I guarantee my sister's been burning up the phone lines since I talked to her this morning. And now that Ronald's got a load of you—"

"You lied to your family."

"Yeah. Sometimes it's fun. Sometimes it's just necessary for survival." He angled his head. "You slipped right into the stream, sweetheart. That accent was a nice touch."

"I got caught up, and I'm not proud of it."

"You might make a good operative. Let me tell you, lying quick and lying well is one of the top requirements of the job."

"And the end justifies the means?"

"Pretty much." It was starting to irritate him, the disapproving ice in her voice. He had the feeling Bailey wasn't nearly as comfortable in gray areas as he was. "We're in, aren't we? And Ronald and Muffy are going to have a rousing success with their little party. So what's the problem?"

"I don't know. I don't like it." A lie, the simple fact of a lie, made her miserably uncomfortable. "One lie just leads to another."

"And enough of them sometimes lead to the truth." He took her bag, opened it and pulled out the velvet pouch, slid the diamond into his hand. "You want the truth, Bailey? Or do you just want honesty?"

"It doesn't seem like there should be a difference." But she took the stone from him. "All right, as you said, we're here. What do you want me to do?"

"Make sure it's real."

"Of course it's real," she said impatiently. "I know it's real."

He merely arched a brow. "Prove it."

With a huffing breath, she turned and headed for a microscope. She employed the dark-field illuminator, adjusting the focus on the binocular microscope with instinctive efficiency.

"Beautiful," she said after a moment, with a tint of reverence in her voice. "Just beautiful."

"What do you see?"

"The interior of the stone. There's no doubt it's of natural origin. The inclusions are characteristic."

"Let's see." He nudged her aside, bent to the microscope himself. "Could be anything."

"No, no. There are no air bubbles. There would be if it was paste, or strass. And the inclusions."

"Doesn't mean anything to me. It's blue, and blue means sapphire."

"Oh for heaven's sake, sapphire is corundum. Do you think I can't tell the difference between carbon and corundum?" She snatched up the stone and marched to another instrument. "This is a polariscope. It tests whether a gem is singly or doubly refracting. As I've already told you, sapphires are doubly refracting, diamonds singly."

She went about her work, muttering to herself, putting her glasses on when she needed them, slipping the eyepiece into the V of her blouse when she didn't. Every move competent, habitual, precise.

Cade tucked his hands in his back pockets, rocked back on his heels and watched.

"Here, the refractometer," she mumbled. "Any idiot can see the refractive index of this stone says diamond, not sapphire." She turned, holding up the stone. "This is a blue diamond, brilliant-cut, weighing 102.6 carats."

"All you need's a lab coat," he said quietly.

"What?"

"You work with this stuff, Bailey. I thought it might be a hobby, but you're too precise, too comfortable. And too easily annoyed when questioned. So my conclusions are that you work with stones, with gems. This type of equipment is as familiar to you as a coffee maker. It's just part of your life."

She lowered her hand and eased herself back onto a stool. "You didn't do all this, go to all this trouble, so we could identify the diamond, did you?"

"Let's just say that was a secondary benefit. Now we have to figure whether you're in the gem or jewelry trade. That's how you got your hands on this." He took the diamond from her, studied it. "And this isn't the kind of thing you see for sale at Westlake or any other jeweler. It's the kind of thing you find in a private collection, or a museum. We've got a really fine museum right here in town. It's called the Smith-

sonian.'' He lowered the stone. ''You may have heard
of it.''

''You think...I took it out of the Smithsonian?''

''I think someone there might have heard of it.''
He slipped the priceless gem casually into his pocket.
''It'll have to wait until tomorrow. They'll be closed.
No, hell, Tuesday.'' He hissed between his teeth.
''Tomorrow's the Fourth, and Monday's a holiday.''

''What should we do until Tuesday?''

''We can start with phone books. I wonder how
many gemologists are in the greater metropolitan
area?''

The reading glasses meant she could pore through
all the books without risking a headache. And pore
through them she did. It was, Bailey thought, something like rereading well-loved fairy tales. It was all
familiar ground, but she enjoyed traveling over it
again.

She read about the history of intaglio cutting in
Mesopotamia, the gems of the Hellenistic period.
Florentine engravings.

She read of famous diamonds. Of the Vargas, the
Jonker, the Great Mogul, which had disappeared cen-
turies before. Of Marie Antoinette and the diamond
necklace some said had cost her her head.

She read technical explanations on gem cutting, on
identification, on optical properties and formations.

They were all perfectly clear to her, and as smooth
as the carnelian tumble stone she worried between her
fingers.

How could it be, she wondered, that she remembered rocks and not people? She could easily identify and discuss the properties of hundreds of crystals and gems. But there was only one single person in the entire world she knew.

And even that wasn't herself.

She only knew Cade. Cade Parris, with his quick, often confusing mind. Cade, with his gentle, patient hands and gorgeous green eyes. Eyes that looked at her as though she could be the focus of his world.

Yet his world was so huge compared to hers. His was populated by people, and memories, places he'd been, things he'd done, moments he'd shared with others.

The huge blank screen that was her past taunted her.

What people did she know, whom had she loved or hated? Had anyone ever loved her? Whom had she hurt or been hurt by? And where had she been, what had she done?

Was she scientist or thief? Lover or loner?

She wanted to be a lover. Cade's lover. It was terrifying how much she wanted that. To sink into bed with him and let everything float away on that warm river of sensation. She wanted him to touch her, really touch her. To feel his hands on her, skimming over naked flesh, heating it, taking her to a place where the past meant nothing and the future was unimportant.

Where there was only now, the greedy, glorious now.

And she could touch him, feel the muscles bunch in his back and shoulders as he covered her. His heart would pound against hers, and she would arch up to meet him, to take him in. And then...

She jumped when the book slapped shut.

"Take a break," Cade ordered, shifting the book across the table where she'd settled to read. "Your eyes are going to fall out of your head."

"Oh, I..." Good God, she thought, goggling at him. She was all but trembling, brutally aroused by her own fantasy. Her pulse was skidding along like skates on bumpy ice. "I was just—"

"Look, you're all flushed."

He turned to get the pitcher of iced tea from the refrigerator, and she rolled her eyes at his back. Flushed? She was flushed? Couldn't the man see she was a puddle just waiting to be lapped up?

He poured her a glass over ice, popped the top on a beer for himself. "We've done enough for one day. I'm thinking steaks on the grill. We'll see if you can put a salad together. Hey." He reached out to steady the glass he'd handed her. "Your hands are shaking. You've been overdoing it."

"No, I..." She could hardly tell him she'd just given serious thought to biting his neck. Carefully she removed her glasses, folded them, set them on the table. "Maybe a little. There's so much on my mind."

"I've got the perfect antidote for overthinking." He took her hand, pulled her to the door and outside, where the air was full of heat and the heady perfume of roses. "A half hour of lazy."

He took her glass, set it on the little wrought-iron table beside the rope hammock, put his beer beside it. "Come on, we'll watch the sky awhile."

He wanted her to lie down with him? Lie down cupped with him in that hammock, while her insides were screaming for release? "I don't think I should—"

"Sure you should." To settle the matter, he gave her a yank and tumbled into the hammock with her. It rocked wildly, making him laugh as she scrambled for balance. "Just relax. This is one of my favorite spots. There's been a hammock here as long as I can remember. My uncle used to nap in this red-and-white striped one when he was supposed to be puttering around the garden."

He slid his arm under her, took one of her nervous hands in his. "Nice and cozy. You can see little pieces of sky through the leaves."

It was cool there, shaded by the maples. She could feel his heart beating steadily when he laid their joined hands on his chest.

"I used to sneak over here a lot. Did a lot of dreaming and planning in this hammock. It was always peaceful over here, and when you were swinging in a hammock in the shade, nothing seemed all that urgent."

"It's like being in a cradle, I suppose." She willed herself to relax, shocked to the core at how much she wanted to roll on top of him and dive in.

"Things are simpler in a hammock." He toyed with her fingers, charmed by their grace and the glitter of rings. He kissed them absently and made her heart turn over in her chest. "Do you trust me, Bailey?"

At that moment, she was certain that, whatever her past, she'd never trusted anyone more. "Yes."

"Let's play a game."

Her imagination whirled into several erotic corners. "Ah…a game?"

"Word association. You empty your mind, and I'll say a word. Whatever pops into your head first, you say it."

"Word association." Unsure whether to laugh or scream, she closed her eyes. "You think it'll jog my memory."

"It can't hurt, but let's just think of it as a lazy game to play in the shade. Ready?"

She nodded, kept her eyes closed and let herself be lulled by the swing of the hammock. "All right."

"City."

"Crowded."

"Desert."

"Sun."

"Work."

"Satisfaction."

"Fire."

"Blue."

When she opened her eyes, started to shift, he snuggled her closer. "No, don't stop and analyze, just let it come. Ready? Love."

"Friends." She let out a breath, found herself relaxing again. "Friends," she repeated.

"Family."

"Mother." She made a small sound, and he soothed it away.

"Happy."

"Childhood."

"Diamond."

"Power."

"Lightning."

"Murder." She let out a choked breath and turned to bury her face against his shoulder. "I can't do this. I can't look there."

"Okay, it's all right. That's enough." He stroked her hair, and though his hand was gentle, his eyes were hot as they stared up through the shady canopy of leaves.

Whoever had frightened her, made her tremble with terror, was going to pay.

While Cade held Bailey under the maple trees, another stood on a stone terrace overlooking a vast estate of rolling hills, tended gardens, jetting fountains.

He was furious.

The woman had dropped off the face of the earth with his property. And his forces were as scattered as the three stars.

It should have been simple. He'd all but had them in his hands. But the bumbling fool had panicked. Or perhaps had simply become too greedy. In either case, he'd let the woman escape, and the diamonds had gone with her.

Too much time had passed, he thought, tapping his small, beautifully manicured hand on the stone railing. One woman vanished, the other on the run, and the third unable to answer his questions.

It would have to be fixed, and fixed soon. The timetable was now destroyed. There was only one person to blame for that, he mused, and stepped back into his lofty office, picked up the phone.

"Bring him to me" was all he said. He replaced the receiver with the careless arrogance of a man used to having his orders obeyed.

Chapter 6

Saturday night. He took her dancing. She'd imagined hunkering down at the kitchen table with books and a pot of strong coffee as soon as dinner was over. Instead, he swept her out of the house, before she'd finished wiping off the counters, barely giving her enough time to run a brush through her hair.

She needed a distraction, he'd told her. She needed music. She needed to experience life.

It was certainly an experience.

She'd never seen anything like it. That she knew. The noisy, crowded club in the heart of Georgetown vibrated with life, shook from floor to ceiling with voices and busy feet. The music was so loud she couldn't hear her own thoughts, and the stingy little table Cade managed to procure for them in the middle of it all was still sticky from the last patron's pitcher of beer.

It astonished her.

Nobody seemed to know anyone else. Or they knew each other well enough to make love standing up in public. Surely the hot, wiggling moves done body against body on the tiny dance floor were nothing less than a mating ritual.

He bought her club soda, stuck to the same harmless drink himself, and watched the show. More, he watched her watch the show.

Lights flashed, voices echoed, and no one seemed to have a care in the world.

"Is this what you usually do on the weekend?" She had to shout into his ear, and she still wasn't certain he would hear her over the crash and din of guitars and drums.

"Now and again." Hardly ever, he thought, studying the ebb and flow of the tide of singles at the bar. Certainly not a great deal since his college days. The idea of bringing her here had been an impulse, even an inspiration, he thought. She could hardly brood and worry under these conditions. "It's a local group."

"I've been duped?" she repeated doubtfully.

"No, no, this band is a local group." He chuckled, scooted his chair closer to hers, slid his arm around her shoulders. "Down-and-dirty rock. No country, no soft crap, no pap. Just kick ass. What do you think?"

She struggled to think, to tune in to the hard, pulsating and repetitive rhythm. Over the driving ocean of music, the band was shouting about dirty deeds and doing them dirt-cheap.

"I don't know, but it sure isn't the 'Ode to Joy.'"

He laughed at that, long and loud, before grabbing her hand. "Come on. Dance with me."

Instant panic. Her palm went damp, her eyes grew huge. "I don't think I know how to—"

"Hell, Bailey. There's not enough room out there to do more than break a couple of Commandments. That doesn't take any practice."

"Yes, but..." He was dragging her toward the dance floor, snaking his way through tables, bumping into people. She lost count of the number of feet they must have trod on. "Cade, I'd rather just watch."

"You're here to experience." He yanked her into his arms, gripped her hips in an intimate and posses-sive way that had her breath locking in her throat. "See? One Commandment down." And suddenly his body was moving suggestively against hers. "The rest is easy."

"I don't think I've ever done this." The lights cir-cling and flashing overhead made her dizzy. Giddy. "I'm sure I'd remember."

He thought she was probably right. There was something entirely too innocent about the way she fumbled, the way the color rushed to her cheeks. He slid his hands over her bottom, up to her waist. "It's just dancing."

"I don't think so. I've probably danced before."

"Put your arms around me." He levered her arms around his neck himself. "And kiss me."

"What?"

"Never mind."

His face was close, and the music was filling her head. The heat from his body, from all the bodies pressed so close against them, was like a furnace. She couldn't breathe, she couldn't think, and when his mouth swooped down on hers, she didn't care.

Her head pounded with the backbeat. It was unmercifully hot, the air thick with smoke and body heat, scented with sweat and liquor and clashing perfumes. All of that faded away. She swayed against him while her lips parted for his and the strong, male essence of him filled her.

"If we'd stayed home, we'd be in bed." He murmured it against her lips, then skimmed his mouth to her ear. She was wearing the perfume he'd bought for her. The scent of it was unreasonably intimate. "I want you in bed, Bailey. I want to be inside you."

She closed her eyes, burrowed against him. Surely no one had said such things to her before. She couldn't have forgotten this wild thrill, this wild fear. Her fingers slipped up into the untidy hair that waved over his collar. "Before, when I was in the kitchen, I—"

"I know." He flicked his tongue over her ear, spread fire everywhere. "I could have had you. Did you think I couldn't see that?" To torment them both, he skimmed his lips along her throat. "That's why we're here instead of home. You're not ready for what I need from you."

"This doesn't make any sense." She thought she murmured it, but he heard her.

"Who the hell cares about sense? This is now." He caught her chin, brought her face to his again. We're now." And kissed her until her blood bubbled and burst in her head. "It can be hot." He bit her bottom lip until she was ready to sink to the floor. "Or sweet." Then laved it tenderly with his tongue. "It can be fun." He spun her out, then whipped her back into his arms with such casual grace that she blinked. "Whatever you want."

Her hands were braced on his shoulders, her face was close to his. Lights revolved around them, and music throbbed. "I think…I think we'd be safer with the fun. For the time being."

"Then let's have it." He whipped her out again, spun her in two fast circles. His eyes lit with amusement when she laughed.

She caught her breath as her body rammed into his again. "You've had lessons."

"Sweetheart, I may have hooked cotillion more times than I want to admit, but some things stuck."

They were moving again, somehow magically, through the thick throng of dancers. "Cotillion? Isn't that white gloves and bow ties?"

"Something like that." He skimmed his hands up her sides, just brushed her breasts. "And nothing like this."

She missed a step, rapped back solidly into what she first took for a steel beam. When she glanced back, she saw what appeared to be one massive muscle with a glossy bald head, a silver nose ring and a gleaming smile.

"I beg your pardon," she began, but found she had breath for nothing else as the muscle whirled her to the right.

She found herself jammed in the middle of a pack of dancers with enthusiastically jabbing elbows and bumping hips. They hooted at her in such a friendly manner, she tried to pick up the beat. She was giggling when she was bumped back into Cade's arms.

"It is fun." Elemental, liberating, nearly pagan. "I'm dancing."

The way her face glowed, her voice rang with delighted laughter, had a grin flashing on his face. "Looks that way."

She waved a hand in front of her face in a useless attempt to fan away the heat. "I like it."

"Then we'll do it again." The volume eased down, the beat smoothed into a hum. "Here comes a slow one. Now all you have to do is plaster yourself all over me."

"I think I already am."

"Closer." His leg slid intimately between hers, his hands cruised low on her hips.

"Oh, God." Her stomach filled with frantic butterflies. "That has to be another Commandment."

"One of my personal favorites."

The music was seductive, sexy and sad. Her mood changed with it, from giddiness to longing. "Cade, I don't think this is smart." But she'd risen to her toes, so their faces were close.

"Let's be reckless. Just for one dance."

"It can't last," she murmured as her cheek pressed against his.

"Shh. For as long as we want."

Forever, she thought, and held tight. "I'm not an empty slate. I've just been erased for a while. Neither of us might like what's written there when we find it."

He could smell her, feel her, taste her. "I know everything I need to know."

She shook her head. "But I don't." She drew back, looked into his eyes. "I don't," she repeated. And when she broke away and moved quickly through the crowd, he let her go.

She hurried into the rest room. She needed privacy, she needed to get her breath back. She needed to remember that, however much she might want it, her life had not begun when she walked into a cramped little office and saw Cade Parris for the first time.

The room was nearly as packed as the dance floor, with women primping at the mirrors, talking about men, complaining about other women. The room smelled thickly of hairspray, perfume and sweat.

In one of the three narrow sinks, Bailey ran the water cold, splashed it on her overheated face. She'd danced in a noisy nightclub and screamed with laughter. She'd let the man she wanted touch her intimately, without a care for who saw it.

And she knew as she lifted her face and studied the reflection in the spotty mirror that none of those things were usual for her.

This was new. Just as Cade Parris was new. And she didn't know how any of it would fit into the life that was hers.

It was happening so quickly, she thought, and dug into her purse for a brush. The purse he'd bought her, the brush he'd bought her, she thought, while emotion swamped her. Everything she had right now, she owed to him.

Was that what she felt for him? A debt, gratitude? Lust?

Not one of the women crowded into the room with her was worried about things like that, she thought. Not one of them was asking herself that kind of question about the man she'd just danced with. The man she wanted, or who wanted her.

They would all go back out and dance again. Or go home. They would make love tonight, if the mood was right. And tomorrow their lives would simply move on.

But she had to ask. And how could she know the answer when she didn't know herself? And how could she take him, or give herself to him, until she did know?

Get yourself in order, she told herself, and methodically ran the brush through her tumbled hair. Time to be sensible, practical. Calm. Satisfied her hair was tidy again, she slipped the brush back into her bag.

A redhead walked in, all legs and attitude, with short-cropped hair and wraparound shades. "Son of a bitch grabbed my butt," she said to no one in particular, and strode into a stall, slammed the door.

Bailey's vision grayed. Clammy waves of dizziness had her clutching the lip of the sink. But her knees went so weak she had to lean over the bowl and gulp for air.

"Hey, hey, you okay?"

Someone patted her on the back, and the voice was like bees buzzing in her head. "Yes, just a little dizzy. I'm all right. I'm fine." Using both hands, she cupped cold water, splashed it again and again on her face.

When she thought her legs would hold her, she snatched paper towels and dried her dripping cheeks. As wobbly as a drunk, she staggered out of the rest room and back into the screaming cave that was the club.

She was bumped and jostled and never noticed. Someone offered to buy her a drink. Some bright soul offered boozily to buy her. She passed through without seeing anything but blinding lights and faceless bodies. When Cade reached her, she was sheet white. Asking no questions, he simply picked her up, to the cheering approval of nearby patrons, and carried her outside.

"I'm sorry. I got dizzy."

"It was a bad idea." He was cursing himself viciously for taking her to a second-rate nightclub with rowdy regulars. "I shouldn't have brought you here."

"No, it was a wonderful idea. I'm glad you brought me. I just needed some air." For the first time, she realized he was carrying her, and wavered between embarrassment and gratitude. "Put me down, Cade. I'm all right."

"I'll take you home."

"No, is there somewhere we can just sit? Just sit and get some air?"

"Sure." He set her on her feet, but watched her carefully. "There's a café just down the street. We can sit outside. Get some coffee."

"Good." She held tightly on to his hand, letting him lead the way. The bass from the band inside the club all but shook the sidewalk. The café a few doors down was nearly as crowded as the club had been, with waiters scurrying to deliver espressos and lattes and iced fruit drinks.

"I came on pretty strong," he began as he pulled out a chair for her.

"Yes, you did. I'm flattered."

Head cocked, he sat across from her. "You're flattered?"

"Yes. I may not remember anything, but I don't think I'm stupid." The air, however close and warm, felt glorious. "You're an incredibly attractive man. And I look around, right here...." Steadying herself, she did just that, scanning the little tables crammed together under a dark green awning. "Beautiful women everywhere. All over the city where we walked today, inside that club, right here in this café. But you came on to me, so I'm flattered."

"That's not exactly the reaction I was looking for, or that I expected. But I guess it'll do for now." He glanced up at the waiter who hustled to their table. "Cappuccino?" he asked Bailey.

"That would be perfect."

"Decaf or regular?" the waiter chirped.

"Real coffee," Cade told him, and leaned closer to Bailey. "Your color's coming back."

"I feel better. A woman came in the ladies' room."

"Did she hassle you?"

"No, no." Touched by his immediate instinct to defend, she laid a hand over his. "I was feeling a little shaky, and then she walked in. Sort of swaggered in." It made her lips curve. "And for a minute, I thought I knew her."

He turned his hand over, gripped hers. "You recognized her?"

"No, not her, precisely, though I thought... No, it was the type, I suppose you'd say. Arrogant, cocky, striking. A tall redhead in tight denim, with a chip on her shoulder." She closed her eyes a moment, let out a long breath, opened them again. "M.J."

"That was the name on the note in your pocket."

"It's there," Bailey murmured, massaging her temples. "It's there somewhere in my head. And it's important. It's vital, but I can't focus on it. But there's a woman, and she's part of my life. And, Cade, something's wrong."

"Do you think she's in trouble?"

"I don't know. When I start to get a picture—when I can almost see her—it's just this image of utter confidence and ability. As if nothing could possibly be wrong. But I know there is something wrong. And it's my fault. It has to be my fault."

He shook his head. Blame wouldn't help. It wasn't the angle they needed to pursue. "Tell me what you see when you start to get that picture. Just try to relax, and tell me.''

"Short, dark red hair, sharp features. Green eyes. But maybe those are yours. But I think hers are green, darker than yours. I could almost draw her face. If I knew how to draw.''

"Maybe you do.'' He took a pen and pad out of his pocket. "Give it a try.''

With her lip caught between her teeth, she tried to capture a sharp, triangular face. With a sigh, she set the pen down as their coffee was served. "I think we can safely assume I'm not an artist.''

"So we'll get one.'' He took the pad back, smiled at the pathetic sketch. "Even I could do better than this, and I scraped by with a C my one dismal semester of art. Do you think you can describe her, the features?''

"I can try. I don't see it all clearly. It's like trying to focus a camera that's not working quite right.''

"Police artists are good at putting things together.''

She slopped coffee over the rim of her cup. "The police? Do we have to go to the police?''

"Unofficial, don't worry. Trust me.''

"I do.'' But the word *police* rang in her head like alarm bells. "I will.''

"We've got something to go on. We know M.J.'s a woman, a tall redhead with a chip on her shoulder. Mary Jane, Martha June, Melissa Jo. You were with her in the desert.''

"She was in the dream.'' Sun and sky and rock.

Contentment. Then fear. "Three of us in the dream, but it won't come clear."

"Well, we'll see if we can put a likeness together, then we'll have somewhere to start."

She stared down into her foamy coffee, thinking her life was just that, a cloud concealing the center. "You make it sound easy."

"It's just steps, Bailey. You take the next step, and see where that goes."

She nodded, stared hard into her coffee. "Why did you marry someone you didn't love?"

Surprised, he leaned back, blew out a breath. "Well, that's quite a change in topic."

"I'm sorry. I don't know why I asked that. It's none of my business."

"I don't know. Under the circumstances, it seems a fair enough question." He drummed his fingers restlessly on the table. "You could say I got tired, worn down by family pressure, but that's a cop-out. Nobody held a gun to my head, and I was over twenty-one."

It annoyed him to admit that, he realized. To be honest with Bailey was to face the truth without excuses. "We liked each other well enough, or at least we did until we got married. A couple of months of marriage fixed that friendship."

"I'm sorry, Cade." It was easy to see the discomfort on his face, his unhappiness with the memory. And though she envied him even that unhappiness, she hated knowing she'd helped put it there. "There's no need to go into it."

"We were good in bed," he went on, ignoring her. And kept his eyes on hers when she shrank back, drew in and away from him. "Right up until the end, the sex was good. The trouble was, toward the end, which was a little under two years from the beginning, it was all heat and no heart. We just didn't give a damn."

Couldn't have cared less, he remembered. Just two bored people stuck in the same house. "That's what it came down to. There wasn't another man, or another woman. No passionate fights over money, careers, children, dirty dishes. We just didn't care. And when we stopped caring altogether, we got nasty. Then the lawyers came in, and it got nastier. Then it was done."

"Did she love you?"

"No." He answered immediately, then frowned, looked hard at nothing and again tried to be honest. And the answer was sad and bruising. "No, she didn't, any more than I loved her. And neither one of us worried about working too hard on that part of it."

He took money from his wallet, dropped it on the table and rose. "Let's go home."

"Cade." She touched his arm. "You deserved better."

"Yeah." He looked at the hand on his arm, the delicate fingers, the pretty rings. "So did she. But it's a little late for that." He lifted her hand so that the ring gleamed between them. "You can forget a lot of things, Bailey, but can you forget love?"

"Don't."

He'd be damned if he'd back off. Suddenly his entire miserable failure of a marriage was slapped into his face. He'd be damned. "If a man put this on your finger, a man you loved, would you forget? Could you?"

"I don't know." She wrenched away, rushed down the sidewalk toward his car. When he whirled her around, her eyes were bright with anger and fears. "I don't *know.*"

"You wouldn't forget. You couldn't, if it mattered. This matters."

He crushed his mouth to hers, pressing her back against the car and battering them both with his frustration and needs. Gone was the patience, the clever heat of seduction. What was left was all the raw demand that had bubbled beneath it. And he wanted her weak and clinging and as desperate as he. For just that moment.

For just the now.

The panic came first, a choke hold that snagged the air from her throat. She couldn't answer this vivid, violent need. Simply wasn't prepared or equipped to meet it and survive.

So she surrendered, abruptly, completely, thoughtlessly, part of her trusting that he wouldn't hurt her. Another praying that he couldn't. She yielded to the flash of staggering heat, the stunning power of untethered lust, rode high on it for one quivering moment.

And knew she might not survive even surrender.

She trembled, infuriating him. Shaming him. He

was hurting her. He almost wanted to, for wouldn't she remember if he did? Wasn't pain easier to remember than kindness?

He knew if she forgot him it would kill him.

And if he hurt her, he would have killed everything worthwhile inside him.

He let her go, stepped back. Instantly she hugged her arms over her chest in a defensive move that slashed at him. Music and voices lifted in excitement and laughter flowed down the sidewalk behind him as he stared at her, spotlighted like a deer caught in headlights.

"I'm sorry."

"Cade—"

He lifted his hands, palms out. His temper rarely flashed, but he knew better than to reach for reason until it had settled again. "I'm sorry," he repeated. "It's my problem. I'll take you home."

And when he had, when she was in her room and the lights were off, he lay out in the hammock, where he could watch her window.

It wasn't so much examining his own life, he realized, that had set him off. He knew the highs and lows of it, the missteps and foolish mistakes. It was the rings on her fingers, and finally facing that a man might have put one of them on her. A man who might be waiting for her to remember.

And it wasn't about sex. Sex was easy. She would have given herself to him that evening. He'd seen it when he walked into the kitchen while she was buried in a book. He'd known she was thinking of him. Wanting him.

Now he thought he'd been a fool for not taking what was there for him. But he hadn't taken it because he wanted more. A lot more.

He wanted love, and it wasn't reasonable to want it. She was adrift, afraid, in trouble neither of them could identify. Yet he wanted her to tumble into love with him, as quickly and completely as he'd tumbled into love with her.

It wasn't reasonable.

But he didn't give a damn about reason.

He'd slay her dragon, whatever the cost. And once he had, he'd fight whoever stood in his way to keep her. Even if it was Bailey herself who stood there.

When he slept, he dreamed. When he dreamed, he dreamed of dragons and black nights and a damsel with golden hair who was locked in a high tower and spun straw into rich blue diamonds.

And when she slept, she dreamed. When she dreamed, she dreamed of lightning and terror and of running through the dark with the power of gods clutched in her hands.

Chapter 7

Despite the fact that she'd slept poorly, Bailey was awake and out of bed by seven. She concluded that she had some internal clock that started her day at an assigned time, and couldn't decide if that made her boring or responsible. In either case, she dressed, resisted the urge to go down the hall and peek into Cade's room and went down to make coffee.

She knew he was angry with her. An icy, simmering anger that she hadn't a clue how to melt or diffuse. He hadn't said a word on the drive back from Georgetown, and the silence had been charged with temper and, she was certain, sexual frustration.

She wondered if she had ever caused sexual frustration in a man before, and wished she didn't feel this inner, wholly female, pleasure at causing it in a man like Cade.

But beyond that, his rapid shift of moods left her baffled and upset. She wondered if she knew any more about human nature than she did of her own past.

She wondered if she knew anything at all about the male of the species.

Did men behave in this inexplicable manner all the time? And if they did, how did a smart woman handle it? Should she be cool and remote until he'd explained himself? Or would it be better if she was friendly and casual, as if nothing had happened?

As if he hadn't kissed her as if he could swallow her whole. As if he hadn't touched her, moved his hands over her, as though he had a right to, as though it were the most natural thing in the world for him to turn her body into a quivering mass of needs.

Now her own mood shifted from timid to annoyed as she wrenched open the refrigerator for milk. How the hell was she supposed to know how to behave? She had no idea if she'd ever been kissed that way before, ever felt this way, wanted this way. Just because she was lost, was she supposed to meekly go in whichever direction Cade Parris pointed her?

And if he pointed her toward the bed, was she supposed to hop in?

Oh, no, she didn't think so. She was a grown woman, capable of making her own decisions. She wasn't stupid and she wasn't helpless. She'd managed to hire herself a detective, hadn't she?

Damn it.

Just because she had no precedents for her own

behavior, that didn't mean she couldn't start setting some here and now.

She would not be a doormat.

She would not be a fool.

She would not be a victim.

She slapped the milk carton down on the counter, scowled out the window. It was Cade's bad luck that she happened to spot him sleeping in the hammock just as her temper peaked.

He wouldn't have dozed so peacefully if he could have seen the way her eyes kindled, the way her lips peeled back in a snarl.

Fueled for battle, Bailey slammed out of the house and marched across the lawn.

She gave the hammock one hard shove.

"Who the hell do you think you are?"

"What?" He shot rudely awake, gripping the sides of the hammock for balance, his brain musty with sleep. "What? Don't you remember?"

"Don't get smart with me." She gave the hammock another shove as he struggled to sit up. "I make my own decisions, I run my own life—such as it is. I hired you to help me find out who I am and what happened to me. I'm not paying you to sulk because I won't hop into bed with you when you have an itch."

"Okay." He rubbed his eyes, finally managed to focus on the stunning and furious face bent over him. "What the hell are you talking about? I'm not sulking, I—"

"Don't tell me you're not sulking," she shot back. "Sleeping out in the backyard like a hobo."

"It's my yard." It irritated him to have to point it out. It irritated him more to be dragged out of sleep into an argument before his mind could engage.

"Taking me dancing," she continued, stalking away and back. "Trying to seduce me on the dance floor, then having a snit because—"

"A snit." That stung. "Listen, sweetheart, I've never had a snit in my life."

"I say you did, and don't call me sweetheart in that tone of voice."

"Now you don't like my tone." His eyes narrowed dangerously, to sharp green slits that threatened retaliation. "Well, let's try a brand-new tone and see how you—" He ended with an oath when she jerked the hammock and flipped him out on his face.

Her first reaction was shock, then an immediate urge to apologize. But as the air turned blue around her, she snapped herself back, jerked her chin up in the air and marched off.

He'd hit the ground with a thud, and he was sure he'd heard his own bones rattle. But he was on his feet again quickly enough, limping a little, but fast enough to snag her before she reached the door.

He yanked her around to face him. "What bug got up your—"

"You deserved it." The blood was roaring in her head, her heart was pounding, but she wasn't going to back down.

"What the hell for?"

"For...whatever."

"Well, that sure covers it."

"Just get out of my way. I'm going for a walk."

"No," he said precisely, "you're not."

"You can't tell me what to do."

He estimated he was close to twice her weight and had a good eight inches in height on her. His lips curved grimly. "Yes, I can. You're hysterical."

That snapped it. "I certainly am not hysterical. If I were hysterical, I'd scratch that nasty smile off your face, and poke those smug eyes out, and—"

To simplify matters, he simply picked her up and carried her inside. She wiggled, sputtered, kicked a little, but he managed to drop her into a kitchen chair. Putting his hands on her shoulders, his face close to hers, he gave one pithy order.

"Stay."

If he didn't have coffee, immediately, he was going to die. Or kill someone.

"You're fired."

"Fine, great, whoopee." He let her fume while he poured coffee and downed it like water. "God, what a way to start the day." He grabbed a bottle of aspirin, fought with the childproof cap while the headache that was brewing insidiously burst into full-blown misery.

"I'm not going to tolerate having a woman yell at me before my eyes are open. Whatever's got you going, sweetheart, you just hold on to it until I—" He cursed again, slamming the stubborn cap on the edge of the counter, where it held firm.

His head was throbbing, his knee wept where it had hit the ground, and he could easily have chewed through the plastic to get to the aspirin.

Swearing ripely, he grabbed a butcher knife out of the wooden block on the counter and hacked at the bottle until he'd decapitated it. His face tight with fury, he turned with the bottle in one hand, the knife in the other. His teeth were clenched.

"Now you listen..." he began.

Bailey's eyes rolled back in her head, and she slid from the chair onto the floor in a dead faint before he could move.

"Sweet God." The knife clattered on the floor, and aspirin rolled everywhere as the mangled bottle hit the tiles. He gathered her up, and for lack of anything better, laid her on the kitchen table while he dampened a cloth. "Come on, Bailey, come around, sweetheart."

He bathed her face, chafed her wrists and cursed himself. How could he have shouted at her that way, manhandled her like that, when she was so fragile? Maybe he'd go out and kick some puppies, stomp on some kittens, for his next act.

When she moaned and shifted, he pressed her limp hand to his lips. "That's the way. All the way back." Her eyes fluttered open while he stroked her hair. "It's okay, Bailey. Take it easy."

"He's going to kill me." Her eyes were open, but blind. She clutched at Cade's shirt as terror strangled her breath. "He's going to kill me."

"No one's going to hurt you. I'm right here."

"He's going to kill me. He's got a knife. If he finds me, he'll kill me."

He wanted to gather her up, soothe it all away, but she'd trusted him to help. He kept his voice very calm, uncurled her fingers from his shirt and held them. "Who's got the knife, Bailey? Who's going to kill you?"

"He...he..." She could see it, almost see it, the hand hacking down, the knife flashing again and again. "There's blood everywhere. Blood everywhere. I have to get away from the blood. The knife. The lightning. I have to run."

He held her still, kept his voice calm. "Where are you? Tell me where you are."

"In the dark. Lights are out. He'll kill me. I have to run."

"Run where?"

"Anywhere." Her breath was coming so fast, the force of it scored her throat like nails. "Anywhere, away. Somewhere away. If he finds me—"

"He's not going to find you. I won't let him find you." He cupped her face firmly in his hands so that her eyes met his. "Slow down now. Just slow down." If she kept panting like that, she was going to hyperventilate and faint on him again. He didn't think he could handle it. "You're safe here. You're safe with me. Understand that?"

"Yes. Yes." She closed her eyes, shuddered hard. "Yes. I need air. Please, I need some air."

He picked her up again, carried her outside. He set her on the padded chaise on the patio, sat beside her.

"Take it slow. Remember, you're safe here. You're safe."

"Yes, all right." With an effort, she evened out the air that seemed to want to clog and burst in her lungs. "I'm all right."

Far from it, he thought. She was sheet white, clammy and shivering. But the memory was close, and he had to try to dislodge it. "No one's going to hurt you. Nothing's going to touch you here. You hang on to that and try to tell me everything you remember."

"It comes in blips." She struggled to breathe past the pressure in her chest. "When you had the knife..." Fear clawed through her again with razored talons.

"I scared you. I'm sorry." He took her hands, held them. "I wouldn't hurt you."

"I know." She closed her eyes again, let the sun beat hot on the lids. "There was a knife. A long blade, curved. It's beautiful. The bone handle is deeply carved. I've seen it—maybe I've used it."

"Where did you see it?"

"I don't know. There were voices, shouting. I can't hear what they're saying. It's like the ocean, all sound, roaring, violent sound." She pressed her hands to her ears, as if she could block it out. "Then there's blood, everywhere there's blood. All over the floor."

"What kind of floor?"

"Carpet, gray carpet. The lightning keeps flashing, the knife keeps flashing."

"Is there a window? Do you see lightning through the window?"

"Yes, I think…" She shivered again, and the scene fighting to form in her mind went blank. "It's dark. Everything went dark, and I have to get away. I have to hide."

"Where do you hide?"

"It's a little place, hardly room, and if he sees, I'll be trapped. He has the knife. I can see it, his hand on the hilt. It's so close, if he turns—"

"Tell me about the hand," Cade said, interrupting her gently. "What does the hand look like, Bailey?"

"It's dark, very dark, but there's a light bouncing around. It almost catches me. He's holding the knife, and his knuckles are white. There's blood on them. On his ring."

"What kind of ring, Bailey?" His eyes stayed intent on her face, but his voice remained calm and easy. "What does the ring look like?"

"It's heavy gold, thick band. Yellow gold. The center stone's a ruby cabochon. On either side there are small diamonds, brilliant-cut. Initials. *T* and *S* in a stylized sweep. The diamonds are red with blood. He's so close, so close, I can smell it. If he looks down. If he looks down and sees me. He'll kill me, slice me to pieces, if he finds me."

"He didn't." Unable to bear it any longer, Cade drew her up, held her. "You got away. How did you get away, Bailey?"

"I don't know." The relief was so huge—Cade's arms around her, the sun warm at her back, his cheek pressed to her hair—she could have wept. "I don't remember."

"It's all right. That's enough."

"Maybe I killed him." She drew back, looked into Cade's face. "Maybe I used the gun that was in the bag and shot him."

"The gun was fully loaded, Bailey."

"I could have replaced it."

"Sweetheart, in my professional opinion, you wouldn't know how."

"But if I—"

"And if you did—" he took her shoulders now, gave her a quick shake "—it was to protect yourself. He was armed, you were terrified, and it sounds as if he'd already killed someone. Whatever you did to survive was right."

She shifted away, looked out over the yard, past the flowers, the leafy old trees, the tidy fence line. "What kind of person am I? There's a very real possibility I saw someone murdered. I did nothing to stop it, nothing to help."

"Be sensible, Bailey. What could you have done?"

"Something," she murmured. "I didn't get to a phone, call the police. I just ran."

"And if you hadn't, you'd be dead." He knew by the way she winced that his tone had been harsh. But it was what she needed. "Instead, you're alive, and bit by bit, we're putting it together."

He rose, paced away, so that he wouldn't give in to the temptation just to cuddle her. "You were in a building of some sort. In a room with gray carpet, probably a window. There was an argument, and someone had a knife. He used it. His initials could be *T.S.* He came after you, and it was dark. More than likely it was a blackout and the building had lost power. A section of North West D.C. lost power for two hours the night before you hired me, so we've got somewhere to look. You knew the building well enough to head for cover. I'd say you belonged there. You live or work there.''

He turned back, noting that she was watching him, paying close attention. Her hands were steady in her lap again. "I can check if there was a knifing reported that night, but I've been watching the papers, and there hasn't been any press on it.''

"But it was days ago now. Someone must have found—found a body, if there was one.''

"Not if it was a private home, or an office that shut down for the long weekend. If there'd been someone else there, other people in the building when it happened, it would have been reported. Odds are you were alone.''

It made his stomach crawl to think of it—Bailey alone in the dark with a killer.

"The storm didn't hit until after ten.''

It was logical, and the simple movement from theory to fact calmed her. "What do we do now?''

"We'll drive around the area that lost power, starting at the hotel where you ended up.''

"I don't remember getting to the hotel, whether I walked or took a cab.''

"You either walked, took a bus or the metro. I've

already checked on cabs. None of the companies dropped off a fare within three blocks of the hotel that night. We're going to move on the assumption that you were on foot, dazed, too shaken to think of hopping a bus, and since the metro only runs until midnight, that's too close to call.''

She nodded, looked down at her hands. "I'm sorry I shouted at you before. You didn't deserve it, after everything you've done for me.''

"I deserved it.'' He tucked his hands in his pockets. "I refuse to accept the term *snit* but I'll allow the phrase *out of sorts.*'' He enjoyed seeing her lips curve in one of her hesitant smiles as she lifted her head.

"I suppose we both were. Did I hurt you when I knocked you down?''

"My ego's going to be carrying a bruise for a while. Otherwise, no.'' He angled his head. There was a quick cockiness in the movement, and in the eyes that glinted at hers. "And I didn't try to seduce you on the dance floor, Bailey. I did seduce you on the dance floor.''

Her pulse stuttered a bit. He was so outrageously gorgeous, standing there in the bright morning sun, rumpled, his dark hair thick and untidy, the dimples denting his cheeks and his mouth arrogantly curved. No woman alive, Bailey thought, could have stopped her mouth from watering.

And she was certain he knew it.

"Your ego seems to function well enough, bruised or not.''

"We can always stage a reenactment.''

Her stomach fluttered at the thought, but she worked up a smile. "I'm glad you're not angry with me anymore. I don't think I handle confrontations very well."

He rubbed his elbow, where he'd lost several layers of skin on impact. "You seemed to do well enough. I'm going to clean up, then we'll take ourselves a Sunday drive."

There were so many kinds of buildings, Bailey thought as Cade tooled around the city. Old ones, new ones, crumbling row houses and refurbished homes. Tall office buildings and squat storefronts.

Had she ever really noticed the city before? she wondered. The sloping stone walls, the trees rising up from the sidewalks. Belching buses with whining air brakes.

Was it always so humid in July? Was the summer sky always the color of paper? And were the flowers always so luscious in the public spaces tucked around statues and along the streets?

Had she shopped in any of these stores, eaten in any of these restaurants?

The trees took over again, tall and stately, lining both sides of the road, so that it seemed they were driving through a park, rather than the middle of a crowded city.

"It's like seeing everything for the first time," she murmured. "I'm sorry."

"Doesn't matter. Something will either click or it won't."

They passed gracious old homes, brick and granite, then another strip of shops, smart and trendy. She made a small sound, and though she was hardly aware of it herself, Cade slowed. "Something click?"

"That boutique. Marguerite's. I don't know."

"Let's take a look." He circled around, back-tracked, then pulled into a narrow lot that fronted several upscale shops. "Everything's closed, but that doesn't mean we can't window shop." Leaning over, he opened her door, then climbed out his own.

"Maybe I just liked the dress in the window," she murmured.

It was very lovely, just a sweep of rose-petal silk with thin straps of glittery rhinestones that continued down to cross under the bodice.

The display was completed by a tiny silver evening bag and impossibly high heels in matching silver.

The way it made her smile, Cade wished the shop was open, so that he could buy it for her. "It's your style."

"I don't know." She cupped her hands to the glass, peered through them for the simple delight of looking at pretty things. "That's a wonderful cocktail suit in navy linen. Oh, and that red dress is just fabulous. Bound to make you feel powerful and accomplished. I really should start wearing bolder colors, but I always wimp out with pastels."

Try this green, Bailey. It's got punch. There's nothing more tiring than a clothes coward.

How long do I have to stand around while you two play with clothes? I'm starving.

Oh, stop bitching. You're not happy unless you're feeding your face or buying new jeans. Bailey, not that tedious beige. The green. Trust me.

"She talked me into it," Bailey murmured. "I bought the green suit. She was right. She always is."

"Who's right, Bailey?" He didn't touch her, afraid that even an encouraging hand on her shoulder would jar her. "Is it M.J.?"

"No, no, not M.J. She's annoyed, impatient, hates to waste time. Shopping's such a waste of time."

Oh, her head hurt. It was going to explode any moment, simply burst off her shoulders. But the need was greater, the need to latch on to this one thing. This one answer. Her stomach rolled, threatened to heave, and her skin went clammy with the effort of holding off nausea.

"Grace." Her voice broke on the name. "Grace," she said again as her knees buckled. "Her name's Grace. Grace and M.J." Tears sprang to her eyes, rolled down her cheeks as she threw her arms around Cade's neck. "I've been here. I've been to this shop. I bought a green suit. I remember."

"Good. Good job, Bailey." He gave her a quick swing.

"No, but that's all." She pressed a hand to her forehead. The pain was screaming now. "That's all I remember. Just being in there with them, buying a suit. It's so foolish. Why should I remember buying a suit?"

"You remember the people." He smoothed his thumbs over her temples. He could all but feel the headache raging inside. "They're important to you. It was a moment, something shared, a happy time."

"But I can't remember them. Not really. Just feelings."

"You're breaking through." He pressed his lips to her brow, drew her back toward the car. "And it's happening quickly now." He eased her down on the seat, hooked her safety belt himself. "And it hurts you."

"It doesn't matter. I need to know."

"It matters to me. We'll get you something for that headache, and some food. Then we'll start again."

Arguments wouldn't sway him. Bailey had to admit that fighting Cade and a blinding headache was a battle she was doomed to lose. She let him prop her up in bed, dutifully swallowed the aspirin he gave her. Obediently she closed her eyes as he instructed, then opened them again when he brought up a bowl of chicken soup.

"It's out of a can," he told her, fussing with the pillows behind her back. "But it should do the job."

"I could eat in the kitchen, Cade. It was a headache, not a tumor. And it's almost gone."

"I'm going to work you hard later. Take the pampering while you can get it."

"All right, I will." She spooned up soup. "It's wonderful. You added thyme."

"For that little hint of France."

Her smile faded. "Paris," she murmured. "Something about Paris.'' The headache snuck back as she tried to concentrate.

"Let it go for now." He sat beside her. "I'd say your subconscious is letting you know you're not all the way ready yet to remember. A piece at a time will do."

"I suppose it'll have to." She smiled again. "Want some soup?"

"Now that you mention it." He leaned forward, let her feed him, and didn't take his eyes from hers. "Not too shabby."

She took another spoonful herself, tasted him. Marvelous. "As handy as you are in the kitchen, I'm surprised your wife let you get away."

"Ex-wife, and we had a cook."

"Oh." She fed him again, slowly taking turns. "I've been trying to figure out how to ask without seeming rude."

He slipped her hair behind her ear. "Just ask."

"Well, this lovely house, the antiques, the fancy sports car... Then there's your office."

His mouth twitched. "Something wrong with my office?"

"No. Well, nothing a bulldozer and a construction crew couldn't cure. It just doesn't compute with the rest."

"I've got a thing about my business paying for itself, and that office is about all it can afford so far. My investigative work pays the bills and just a little more. On a personal level, I'm rolling in it." His eyes laughed into hers. "Money, that is. If that's what you're asking."

"I guess it was. You're rich, then."

"Depends on your definition, or if you mean me personally or the entire family. It's shopping centers, real estate, that sort of thing. A lot of doctors and lawyers and bankers down through the ages. And me, I'm—"

"The black sheep," she finished for him, thrilled that he was just that. "You didn't want to go into the family business. You didn't want to be a doctor or a lawyer or a banker."

"Nope. I wanted to be Sam Spade."

Delighted, she chuckled. "*The Maltese Falcon.* I'm glad you didn't want to be a banker."

"Me, too." He took the hand she'd laid on his cheek, pressed his lips to it and felt her quiver of response.

"I'm glad I found your name in the phone book." Her voice thickened. "I'm glad I found you."

"So am I." He took the tray from between them, set it aside. Even if he'd been blind, he thought, he would have understood what was in her eyes just then. And his heart thrilled to it. "I could walk out of here and leave you alone now." He trailed a finger across her collarbone, then let it rest on the pulse that beat rabbit-quick at her throat. "That's not what I want to do."

It was her decision, she knew. Her choice. Her moment. "That's not what I want, either." When he cupped her face in his hands, she closed her eyes. "Cade, I may have done something horrible."

His lips paused an inch from hers. "I don't care."

"I may have— I may be—" Determined to face it, she opened her eyes again. "There may be someone else."

His fingers tightened. "I don't give a damn."

She let out a long breath, and took her moment. "Neither do I," she said, and pulled him to her.

Chapter 8

This was what it felt like to be pressed under a man's body. A man's hard, needy body. A man who wanted you above all else.

For that moment.

It was breathless and stunning, exciting and fresh. The way he combed his fingers through her hair as his lips covered hers thrilled her. The fit of mouth against mouth, as if the only thing lips and tongues were made for were to taste a lover. And it was the taste of him that filled her—strong and male and real.

Whatever had come before, whatever came after, this mattered now.

She stroked her hands over him, and it was glorious. The shape of his body, the breadth of shoulders, the length of back, the narrowing of waist, the muscles beneath so firm, so tight. And when her hands skimmed under his shirt, the smooth, warm flesh beneath fascinated.

"Oh, I've wanted to touch you." Her lips raced over his face. "I was afraid I never would."

"I've wanted you from the first moment you walked in the door." He drew back only enough to see her eyes, the deep, melting brown of them. "Before you walked in the door. Forever."

"It doesn't make any sense. We don't—"

"It doesn't matter. Only this." His lips closed over hers again, took the kiss deeper, tangling their flavors together.

He wanted to go slowly, draw out every moment. It seemed he'd waited for her all his life, so now he could take all the time in the world to touch, to taste, to explore and exploit. Each shift of her body beneath his was a gift. Each sigh a treasure.

To have her like this, with the sun streaming through the window, with her hair flowing gold over the old quilt and her body both yielding and eager, was sweeter than any dream.

They belonged. It was all he had to know.

To see her, to unfasten the simple shirt he'd picked for her, to open it inch by inch to pale, smooth flesh was everything he wanted. He skimmed his fingertips over the curve of her breast, felt her skin quiver in response, watched her eyes flicker dark, then focus on his.

"You're perfect." He cupped her, and she was small and firm and made for his palm.

He bent his head, rubbed his lips where the lace of

her bra met flesh, then moved them up, lazily up her throat, over her jaw, and back to nip at her mouth.

No one had kissed her like this before. She knew it was impossible for anyone else to have taken such care. With a soft sigh, she poured herself into the kiss, murmuring when he shifted her to slip the shirt away, trembling when he slid the lace aside and bared her breasts to his hands.

And his mouth.

She moaned, lost, gloriously lost, in a dark maze of sensations. Soft here, then rough, cool, then searing, each feeling bumped gently into the next, then merged into simple pleasure. Whichever way she turned, there was something new and thrilling. When she tugged his shirt away, there was the lovely slippery slide of his flesh against hers, the intimacy of it, heart to heart.

And her heart danced to the play of his lips, the teasing nip of teeth, the slow torture of tongue.

The air was like syrup, thick and sweet, as he slid her slacks over her hips. She struggled to gulp it in, but each breath was shallow and short. He was touching her everywhere, his hands slick and slow, but relentlessly pushing her higher and stronger until the heat was immense. It kindled inside her like a brush fire.

She moaned out his name, clutching the quilt and dragging it into tangles as her body strained to reach for something just beyond her grasp. As she arched desperately against him, he watched her. Slid up her body again until his lips were close to hers, and watched her. Watched her as, with quick, clever fingers, he tore her free.

It was his name she called when the heat reached flash point, and his body she clung to as her own shuddered.

That was what he'd wanted.

His name was still vibrating on her lips when he crushed them with his, when he rolled with her over the bed in a greedy quest to take and possess. Blind with need, he tugged at his jeans, trembling himself when she buried her mouth against his throat, strained against him in quivering invitation.

She was more generous than any fantasy. More generous than any wish. More his than any dream.

With sunlight pouring over the tangled sheets, she arched to him, opened as if she'd been waiting all her life for him. His heart pounded in his head as he slipped inside her, moved to fill her.

Shock froze him for a dazed instant, and every muscle tensed. But she shook her head, wrapped herself around him and took him in.

"You" was all she said. "Only you."

He lay still, listening to her heart thudding, absorbing the quakes of her body with his. Only him, he thought, and closed his eyes. She'd been innocent. Untouched. A miracle. And his heart was tugged in opposing directions of guilt and pure selfish pleasure.

She'd been innocent, and he'd taken her.

She'd been untouched, until he touched.

He wanted to beg her to forgive him.

He wanted to climb out on the roof and crow.

Not certain either would suit the situation, he gently tested the waters.

"Bailey?"

"Hmm?"

"Ah, in my professional opinion as a licensed investigator, I conclude it's extremely unlikely you're married." He felt the rumble of her laughter, and lifted his head to grin down at her. "I'll put it in my report."

"You do that."

He brushed the hair from her cheek. "Did I hurt you? I'm sorry. I never considered—"

"No." She pressed her hand over his. "You didn't hurt me. I'm happy, giddy. Relieved." Her lips curved on a sigh. "I never considered, either. I'd say we were both surprised." Abruptly her stomach fluttered with nerves. "You're not...disappointed? If you—"

"I'm devastated. I really hoped you'd be married, with six kids. I really only enjoy making love with married women."

"No, I meant... Was it—was I—was everything all right?"

"Bailey." On a half laugh, he rolled over so that she could settle on his chest. "You're perfect. Absolutely, completely perfect. I love you." She went very still, and her cheek stayed pressed to his heart. "You know I do," he said quietly. "From the moment I saw you."

Now she wanted to weep, because it was everything she wanted to hear, and nothing she could accept. "You don't know me."

"Neither do you."

She lifted her head, shook it fiercely. "That's exactly the point. Joking about it doesn't change the truth."

"Here's the truth, then." He sat up, took her firmly by the shoulders. "I'm in love with you. In love with the woman I'm holding right now. You're exactly what I want, what I need, and sweetheart—" he kissed her lightly "—I'm keeping you."

"You know it's not that simple."

"I'm not asking for simple." He slid his hands down, gripped hers. "I'm asking you to marry me."

"That's impossible." Panicked, she tugged on her hands, but he gripped them calmly and held her in place. "You know that's impossible. I don't know where I come from, what I've done. I met you three days ago."

"That all makes sense, or would, except for one thing." He drew her against him and shot reason to hell with a kiss.

"Don't do this." Torn to pieces, she wrapped her arms around his neck, held tight. "Don't do this, Cade. Whatever my life was, right now it's a mess. I need to find the answers."

"We'll find the answers. I promise you that. But there's one I want from you now." He drew her head back. He'd expected the tears, knew they'd be shimmering in her eyes and turning them deep gold. "Tell me you love me, Bailey, or tell me you don't."

"I can't—"

"Just one question," he murmured. "You don't need a yesterday to answer it."

No, she needed nothing but her own heart. "I can't tell you I don't love you, because I can't lie to you." She shook her head, pressed her fingers to his lips before he could speak. "I won't tell you I do, because it wouldn't be fair. It's an answer that has to wait until I know all the others. Until I know who the woman is who'll tell you. Give me time."

He'd give her time, he thought when her head was nestled on his shoulder again. Because nothing and no one was taking her from him, whatever they found on the other side of her past.

Cade liked to say that getting to a solution was just a matter of taking steps. Bailey wondered how many more there were left to climb. She felt she'd rushed up a very long staircase that day, and when reaching the landing been just as lost as ever.

Not entirely true, she told herself as she settled down at the kitchen table with a notepad and pencil. Even the urge to make a list of what she knew indicated that she was an organized person, and one who liked to review things in black and white.

Who is Bailey?

A woman who habitually rose at the same hour daily. Did that make her tedious and predictable, or responsible? She liked coffee black and strong, scrambled eggs, and her steaks medium rare. Fairly ordinary tastes. Her body was trim, not particularly muscular, and without tan lines. So, she wasn't a fitness fanatic or a sun-worshiper. Perhaps she had a job that kept her indoors.

Which meant, she thought with some humor, she wasn't a lumberjack or a lifeguard.

She was a right-handed, brown-eyed blonde, and was reasonably sure her hair color was natural or close to what she'd been born with.

She knew a great deal about gemstones, which could mean they were a hobby, a career, or just something she liked to wear. She had possession of a diamond worth a fortune that she'd either stolen, bought—highly unlikely, she thought—or gained through an accident of some sort.

She'd witnessed a violent attack, possibly a murder, and run away.

Because that fact made her temple start to throb again, she skipped over it.

She hummed classical music in the shower and liked to watch classic film noir on television. And she couldn't figure out what that said about her personality or her background.

She liked attractive clothes, good materials, and shied away from strong colors unless pushed.

It worried her that she might be vain and frivolous.

But she had at least two female friends who shared part of her life. Grace and M.J., M.J. and Grace. Bailey wrote the names on the pad, over and over, hoping that the simple repetition would strike a fresh spark.

They mattered to her, she could feel that. She was frightened for them and didn't know why. Her mind might be blank, but her heart told her that they were special to her, closer to her than anyone else in the world.

But she was afraid to trust her heart.

There was something else she knew that Bailey didn't want to write down, didn't want to review in black and white.

She'd had no lover. There'd been no one she cared for enough, or who cared for her enough, for intimacy. Perhaps in the life she led she'd been too judgmental, too intolerant, too self-absorbed, to accept a man into her bed.

Or perhaps she'd been too ordinary, too boring, too undesirable, for a man to accept her into his.

In any case, she had a lover now.

Why hadn't the act of lovemaking seemed foreign to her, or frightening, as it seemed it would to the uninitiated? Instead, with Cade, it had been as natural as breathing.

Natural, exciting and perfect.

He said he loved her, but how could she believe it? He knew only one small piece of her, a fraction of the whole. When her memory surfaced, he might find her to be the very type of woman he disliked.

No, she wouldn't hold him to what he'd said to this Bailey, until she knew the whole woman.

And her feelings? With a half laugh, she set the pencil aside. She'd been drawn to him instantly, trusted him completely the moment he took her hand. And fallen in love with him while she watched him stand in this kitchen, breaking brown eggs into a white bowl.

But her heart couldn't be trusted in this case, either. The closer they came to finding the truth, the closer they came to the time when they might turn from each other and walk away.

However much she wished it, they couldn't leave the canvas bag and its contents in his safe, forget they existed and just be.

"You forgot some things."

She jolted, turned her head quickly and looked into his face. How long, she wondered, had he been standing behind her, reading her notes over her shoulder, while she was thinking of him?

"I thought it might help me to write down what I know."

"Always a good plan." He walked to the fridge, took out a beer, poured her a glass of iced tea.

She sat feeling foolish and awkward, her hands clutched in her lap. Had they really rolled naked on a sun-washed bed an hour before? How was such intimacy handled in a tidy kitchen over cold drinks and puzzles?

He didn't seem to have a problem with it. Cade sat across from her, propped his feet on an empty chair and scooted her pad over. "You're a worrier."

"I am?"

"Sure." He flipped a page, started a new list. "You're worrying right now. What should you say to this guy, now that you're lovers? Now that you know he's wildly in love with you, wants to spend the rest of his life with you?''

"Cade—"

"Just stating the facts.'' And if he stated them often enough, he figured she'd eventually accept them. "The sex was great, and it was easy. So you worry about that, too. Why did you let this man you've known for a weekend take you to bed, when you've never let another man get that close?'' His eyes flicked up, held hers. "The answer's elementary. You're just as wildly in love with me, but you're afraid to face it.''

She picked up her glass, cooled her throat. "I'm a coward?''

"No, Bailey, you're not a coward, but you're constantly worried that you are. You're a champion worrier. And a woman, I think, who gives herself very little credit for her strengths, and has very little tolerance for her weaknesses. Self-judgmental.''

He wrote that down, as well, while she frowned at the words on the page. "It seems to me someone in my situation has to try to judge herself.''

"Practical, logical.'' He continued the column. "Now, leave the judging to me a moment. You're compassionate, responsible, organized. And a creature of habit. I'd say you hold some sort of position that requires those traits, as well as a good intellect. Your work habits are disciplined and precise. You also have a fine aesthetic sense.''

"How can you be so sure?''

"Bailey, forgetting who you are doesn't change

who you are. That's your big flaw in reasoning here.
If you hated brussels sprouts before, it's likely you're
still going to hate them. If you were allergic to cats,
you're still going to sneeze if you pet a kitten. And
if you had a strong, moral and caring heart, it's still
beating inside you. Now let me finish up here.''

She twisted her head, struggling to read upside
down. ''What are you putting down?''

''You're a lousy drinker. Probably a metabolism
thing. And I think at this point, we could have some
wine later, so I can take full advantage of that.'' He
grinned over at her. ''And you blush. It's a sweet,
old-fashioned physical reaction. You're tidy. You
hang up your towels after you shower, you rinse off
your dishes, you make your bed every morning.''

There were other details, he thought. She wiggled
her foot when she was nervous, her eyes went gold
when she was aroused, her voice turned chilly when
she was annoyed.

''You've had a good education, probably up north,
from your speech pattern and accent. I'd say you concentrated on your studies like a good girl and didn't
date much. Otherwise you wouldn't have been a vir-
gin up to a couple hours ago. There, you blushed
again. I really love when you do that.''

''I don't see the point in this.''

''There's that cool, polite tone. Indulge me,'' he
added, then sipped his beer. ''You've got a slim body,
smooth skin. You either take care of both or you were
lucky genetically. By the way, I like your unicorn.''

She cleared her throat. ''Thank you.''

"No, thank you," he said, and chuckled. "Anyway, you have or make enough money to afford good clothes. Those classic Italian pumps you were wearing go for about two hundred and fifty at department-store prices. And you had silk underwear. I'd say the silk undies and the unicorn follow the same pattern. You like to be a little daring under the traditional front."

She was just managing to close her gaping mouth. "You went through my clothes? My underwear?"

"What there was of them, and all in the name of investigation. Great underwear," he told her. "Very sexy, simple, and pricey. I'd say peach silk ought to look terrific on you."

She made a strangled sound, fell back on silence. There was really nothing to say.

"I don't know the annual income of your average gemologist or jewelry designer—but I'll lay odds you're one or the other. I'm leaning toward the scientist as vocation, and the designer as avocation."

"That's a big leap, Cade."

"No, it's not. Just another step. The pieces are there. Wouldn't you think a diamond like the one in the safe would require the services of a gemologist? Its authenticity would have to be verified, its value assessed. Just the way you verified and assessed it yesterday."

Her hands trembled, so she put them back in her lap. "If that's true, then it ups the likelihood that I stole it."

"No, it doesn't." Impatient with her, he tapped the

pencil sharply against the pad. "Look at the other facts. Why can't you see yourself? You wouldn't steal a stick of gum. Doesn't the fact that you're riddled with guilt over the very thought you might have done something illegal give you a clue?"

"The fact is, Cade, I have the stone."

"Yeah, and hasn't it occurred to you, in that logical, responsible, ordered mind of yours, that you might have been protecting it?"

"Protecting it? From—"

"From whoever killed to get their hands on it. From whoever would have killed you if he had found you. That's what plays, Bailey, that's what fits. And if there are three stones, then you might very well know where the others are, as well. You may be protecting all of them."

"How?"

He had some ideas on that, as well, but didn't think she was ready to hear them. "We'll work on that. Meanwhile, I've made a few calls. We've got a busy day ahead of us tomorrow. The police artist will come over in the morning, see if she can help you put images together. And I managed to snag one of the undercurators, or whatever they're called, at the Smithsonian. We have a one-o'clock appointment tomorrow."

"You got an appointment on a holiday?"

"That's where the Parris name and fortune come in handy. Hint at funding, and it opens a lot of musty old doors. And we'll see if that boutique opens for the holiday sale hunters, and find out if anyone re-members selling a green suit.''

"It doesn't seem like we're doing enough.''

"Sweetheart, we've come a long way in a short time.''

"You're right.'' She rose, walked to the window. There was a wood thrush in the maple tree, singing its heart out. "I can't begin to tell you how grateful I am.''

"I'll bill you for the professional services,'' he said shortly. "And I don't want gratitude for the rest of it.''

"I have to give it, whether or not you take it. You made this bearable, more than that. I don't know how many times you made me smile or laugh or just forget it all for little spaces of time. I think I'd have gone crazy without you, Cade.''

"I'm going to be there for you, Bailey. You're not going to be able to shake me loose.''

"You're used to getting what you want,'' she mur-mured. "I wonder if I am. It doesn't feel as if that's true.''

"That's something you can change.''

He was right. That was a matter of patience, per-severance, control. And perhaps wanting the right things. She wanted him, wanted to think that one day she could stand here, listening to the wood thrush sing of summer while Cade drowsed in the hammock. It could be their house instead of his. Their life. Their family.

If it was the right thing, and she could persevere.

"I'm going to make you a promise." She followed the impulse and turned, letting her heart be reckless. He was so much what she needed, sitting there with his jeans torn at the knee, his hair too long, his feet bare. "If, when this is over, when all the steps have been taken, all the pieces are in place to make the whole...if I can and you still want me, I'll marry you."

His heart stuttered in his chest. Emotion rose up to fill his throat. Very carefully, he set the bottle aside, rose. "Tell me you love me."

It was there, in her heart, begging to be said. But she shook her head. "When it's all over, and you know everything. If you still want me."

"That's not the kind of promise that suits me. No qualifications, Bailey. No whens, no ifs. Just you."

"It's all I can give you. It's all I have."

"We can go into Maryland on Tuesday, get a license. Be married in a matter of days."

He could see it. The two of them, giddy in love, rousing some sleepy-eyed country J.P. out of bed in the middle of the night. Holding hands in the living room while an old yellow dog slept on a braid rug, the J.P.'s wife played the piano and he and the woman he loved exchanged vows.

And sliding the ring onto her finger, feeling her slide one on his, was the link that would bind them.

"There are no blood tests in Maryland," he continued. "Just a couple of forms, and there you are."

He meant it. It staggered her to see in those deep green eyes that he meant nothing less than he said.

He would take her exactly as she was. He would love her just as she stood.

How could she let him?

"And what name would I put on the form?"

"It doesn't matter. You'll have mine." He gripped her arms, drew her against him. In all his life, there had been no one he needed as much. "Take mine."

Just take, she thought when his lips covered hers. Take what was offered—the love, the safety, the promise. Let the past come as it would, let the future drift, and seize the moment.

"You know it wouldn't be right." She pressed her cheek to his. "You need to know as much as I do."

Maybe he did. However much the fantasy of a reckless elopement appealed, creating a fake identity for Bailey, it wasn't the answer either one of them needed. "Could be fun." He struggled to lighten the mood. "Like practice for the real thing." He pulled her back to arm's length, studied her face. Delicate, troubled. Lovely. "You want orange blossoms, Bailey? A white dress and organ music?"

Because her heart sighed at the image, she managed to smile. "I think I might. I seem to be a traditional soul."

"Then I should buy you a traditional diamond."

"Cade—"

"Just speculating," he murmured, and lifted her left hand. "No, however traditional your soul, your taste in jewelry is unique. We'll find something that suits. But I should probably take you to meet the family.'' His eyes lifted to hers, and he laughed. "God help you.''

Just a game, she thought, just pretend. She smiled back at him. "I'd love to meet your family. See Camilla do pirouettes in her tutu.''

"If you can get through that and still want to marry me, I'll know you're hopelessly in love with me. They'll put you through the gauntlet, sweetheart. A very sophisticated, silk-edged gauntlet. Where did you go to school, what does your father do, does your mother play bridge or tennis? And by the way, what clubs do you belong to, and did I run into you on the slopes last season at St. Moritz?''

Instead of making her unhappy, it made her laugh. "Then I'd better find out the answers.''

"I like making them up. I took a cop to Muffy's tenth-anniversary bash. Couldn't get out of it. We told everyone she was the niece of the Italian prime minister, educated in a Swiss boarding school and interested in acquiring a pied-à-terre in D.C.''

Her brows drew together. "Oh, really?''

"They all but drooled on her. Not nearly the reaction we'd have gotten with the truth.''

"Which was?''

"She was a uniformed cop who grew up in New York's Little Italy and transferred to Washington after her divorce from a guy who ran a pasta place off Broadway.''

"Was she pretty?''

"Sure.'' His grin flashed. "Gorgeous. Then there was the lounge singer in Chevy Chase who—''

"I don't think I want to know." She turned away, picked up her empty glass and made a business out of rinsing it out. "You've dated a lot of women, I suppose."

"That depends on your definition of 'a lot.' I could probably run a list of names, ages, physical descriptions and last known addresses. Want to type it up for me?"

"No."

Delighted, he nuzzled the back of her neck. "I've only asked one woman to marry me."

"Two," she corrected, and set the now sparkling glass on the counter with a snap.

"One. I didn't ask Carla. That just sort of evolved. And now she's happily married—as far as I can tell—to a corporate lawyer and the proud mama of a bouncing baby girl named Eugenia. So it hardly counts, anyway."

She bit her lip. "You didn't want children?"

"Yes, I did. I do." He turned her around, kissed her gently. "But we're not naming any kid of ours Eugenia. Now what do you say we think about going out for dinner, someplace quiet, where we can neck at the table? Then we can watch the fireworks."

"It's too early for dinner."

"That's why I said we should think about it." He scooped her up. "First we have to go upstairs and make love again."

Her pulse gave a pleasant little jump as she curled her arms around his neck. "We have to?"

''It'll pass the time. Unless you'd rather play gin rummy?''

Chuckling, she traced a line of kisses up his neck. ''Well, if those are my only choices...''

''Tell you what, we can play strip gin rummy. We can both cheat and that way— Hell.'' He was halfway up the stairs with her, and nicely aroused, when the doorbell sounded. ''Hold that thought, okay?'' He set her down, and went to answer.

One peek through the side panel of wavy glass framing the door had him groaning. ''Perfect timing, as always.'' With a hand on the knob, he turned, looked at Bailey. ''Sweetheart, the woman on the other side of this door is my mother. I realize you expressed a mild interest in meeting my family, but I'm giving you this chance, because I love you. I really do. So I'm advising you to run, hide, and don't look back.''

Nerves fluttered, but she straightened her shoulders. ''Stop being silly and open the door.''

''Okay, but I warned you.'' Bracing himself, he pulled the door open and fixed a bright, welcoming smile on his face. ''Mother.'' As was expected, he kissed her smooth, polished cheek. ''What a nice surprise.''

''I wouldn't have to surprise you if you'd ever return my calls.'' Leona Parris stepped into the foyer.

She was, Bailey realized with a stunned first glance, a striking woman. Surely, with three grown children and several grandchildren, she had to be at least fifty. She could have passed for a sleek thirty-five.

Her hair was a lush sable brown with hints of golden highlights and fashioned in a perfect and elegant French twist that complemented a face of ivory and cream, with cool green eyes, straight nose and sulky mouth. She wore an elegant tailored bronze-toned suit that nipped at her narrow waist.

The topaz stones at her ears were square-cut and big as a woman's thumb and earned Bailey's instant admiration.

"I've been busy," Cade began. "A couple of cases, and some personal business."

"I certainly don't want to hear about your cases, as you call them." Leona set her leather bag on the foyer table. "And whatever your personal business is, it's no excuse for neglecting your family duties. You put me in a very awkward position with Pamela. I had to make your pathetic excuses."

"You wouldn't have had to make excuses if you hadn't set it up in the first place." He could feel the old arguments bubbling inside him, and he struggled not to fall into the familiar, too-predictable traps. "I'm sorry it put you in an awkward position. Do you want some coffee?"

"What I want, Cade, is an explanation. At Muffy's garden party yesterday—which you also failed to attend—Ronald told me some wild tale about you being engaged to some woman I've never heard of with a connection to the Princess of Wales."

"Bailey." Because he'd all but forgotten her, Cade

turned, offered an apologetic smile and held out a hand. "Bailey, come meet my mother."

Oh, good God, was all that came into Bailey's head as she descended the stairs.

"Leona Parris, meet Bailey, my fiancée."

"Mrs. Parris." Bailey's voice trembled a bit as she offered a hand. "How wonderful to meet you. Cade has told me so much about you."

"Really?" Attractive, certainly, Leona mused. Well-groomed, if a bit understated. "He's told me virtually nothing about you, I'm afraid. I don't believe I caught your full name."

"Bailey's only been in the States for a few months." Cade barreled in, all cheer and delight. "I've been keeping her to myself." He slipped an arm around Bailey's shoulders, squeezed possessively. "We've had a whirlwind courtship, haven't we, sweetheart?"

"Yes," Bailey said faintly. "A whirlwind. You could say that."

"And you're a jewelry designer." Lovely rings, Leona noted. Unique and attractive. "A distant cousin of the Princess of Wales."

"Bailey doesn't like to drop names," Cade said quickly. "Sweetheart, maybe you ought to make those calls. Remember the time difference in London."

"Where did you meet?" Leona demanded.

Bailey opened her mouth, struggling to remember if they'd spun this part of the lie for Ronald. "Actually—"

"At the Smithsonian," Cade said smoothly. "In front of the Hope Diamond. I was researching a case, and Bailey was sketching designs. She looked so intent and artistic. It took me twenty minutes of fast talking and following her around—remember how you threatened to call the security guard, sweetheart? But I finally charmed her into having a cup of coffee with me. And speaking of coffee—"

"This is just ridiculous," Bailey said, interrupting him. "Absolutely ridiculous. Cade, this is your mother, and I'm just not having it." She turned, faced Leona directly. "We did not meet in the Smithsonian, and the Princess of Wales is not my cousin. At least I seriously doubt it. I met Cade on Friday morning, when I went to his office to hire him. I needed a private investigator because I have amnesia, a blue diamond and over a million dollars in cash."

Leona waited ten humming seconds while her foot tapped. Then her lips firmed. "Well, I can see neither of you intends to tell the simple truth. As you prefer to make up outrageous fabrications, I can only presume that you're perfectly suited to one another."

She snatched up her bag and marched to the door with outraged dignity in every step. "Cade, I'll wait to hear from you when you decide to grant me the courtesy of the simple truth."

While Bailey simply stared, Cade grinned like a fool at the door his mother had closed with a snap.

"I don't understand. I did tell her the truth."

"And now I know what they mean by 'the truth shall set you free.'" He let out a whooping laugh, swung her back up into his arms. "She's so ticked off now she'll leave me alone for a week. Maybe two." He gave Bailey an enthusiastic kiss as he headed for the stairs. "I'm crazy about you. Who would have thought telling her the real story would have gotten her off my back?"

Still laughing, he carried her into the bedroom and dropped her on the mattress. "We've got to celebrate. I've got some champagne chilled. I'm going to get you drunk again."

Pushing her hair out of her face, she sat up. "Cade, she's your mother. This is shameful."

"No, it's survival." He leaned over, gave her a smacking kiss this time. "And, sweetheart, we're both black sheep now. I can't tell you how much more fun that's going to be for me."

"I don't think I want to be a black sheep," she called as he headed out again.

"Too late." His laughter echoed back to her.

Chapter 9

They did make it out to dinner. But they settled for grilled burgers and potatoes fried in peanut oil at a country fair in rural Maryland. He'd thought about a romantic little restaurant, then a fight through the teeming crowds downtown for the huge fireworks display.

Then inspiration had struck. Ferris wheels and shooting galleries. Live music, whirling lights, the flash of fireflies in a nearby field, with fireworks to top it off.

It was, he thought, the perfect first date.

When he told her just that, while she clung to him with screams locked in her throat on the whizzing car of the Tilt-A-Whirl, she laughed, shut her eyes tight and hung on for her life.

He wanted to ride everything, and he pulled her

along from line to line, as eager as any of the children tugging on an indulgent parent's hand. She was spun, shaken, twirled and zoomed until her head revolved and her stomach flopped.

Then he tilted her face upward for inspection, declared that since she wasn't turning green yet they could do it all again.

So they did.

"Now, you need a prize," he decided as she staggered off the Octopus.

"No more cotton candy. I'm begging you."

"I was thinking more of an elephant." He hooked an arm around her waist and headed toward the shooting gallery. "That big purple one up there."

It was three feet tall, with a turned-up trunk and toenails painted a bright pink. An elephant. The thought of elephants made her smile bloom brilliantly.

"Oh, it's wonderful." She grinned, fluttered her lashes at Cade. "I want it."

"Then it's my job to get it for you. Just stand back, little lady." He plunked down bills, chose his weapon. Cheery-faced rabbits and ducks rolled by, with the occasional wolf or bear rearing up at odd moments to threaten. Cade sighted the air gun and fired.

Bailey grinned, then applauded, then gaped as wildlife died in droves. "You didn't miss once." She goggled at him. "Not once."

Her wide-eyed admiration made him feel like a teenager showing off for the prom queen. "She wants the elephant,'' he told the attendant, then laughed when she launched herself into his arms.

''Thank you. You're wonderful. You're amazing.''

Since each statement was punctuated by eager kisses, he thought she might like the floppy-eared brown dog, as well. ''Want another?''

''Man, you're killing me here,'' the attendant muttered, then sighed as Cade pulled out more bills.

''Want to give it a try?'' Cade offered the rifle to Bailey.

''Maybe.'' She bit her lip and studied her prey. It had looked simple enough when Cade did it. ''All right.''

''Just sight through the little V at the end of the barrel,'' he began, stepping behind her to adjust her stance.

''I see it.'' She held her breath and pulled the trigger. The little pop had her jolting, but the ducks swam on, and the rabbits continued to hop. ''Did I miss?''

''Only by a mile or so.'' And he was dead certain the woman had never held a gun in her life. ''Try again.''

She tried again, and again. By the time she'd managed to nip a few feathers and ruffle some fur, Cade had put twenty dollars back in the attendant's grateful hands.

''It looked so easy when you did it.''

''That's okay, sweetheart, you were getting the hang of it. What'd she win?''

The attendant perused his lowest row of prizes,

generally reserved for children under twelve, and came up with a small plastic duck.

"I'll take it." Delighted, she tucked it in the pocket of her slacks. "My first trophy."

With hands linked, they strolled the midway, listening to the screams, the distant music of a bluegrass band, the windy whirl of rides. She loved the lights, the carnival colors, bright as jewels in the balmy night. And the smells of frying oil, of spun sugar and spiced sauces.

It seemed so easy, as if there couldn't be any trouble in the world—only lights and music and laughter.

"I don't know if I've ever been to a country carnival before," she told him. "But if I have, this one is the best."

"I still owe you a candlelight dinner."

She turned her head to smile at him. "I'll settle for another ride on the Ferris wheel."

"Sure you're up to it?"

"I want to go around again. With you."

She stood in line, flirted with a toddler who kept his head on his father's shoulder and peeked at her with huge blue eyes. She wondered if she was good with children, if she'd ever had a chance to be. And, laying her head on Cade's shoulder, dreamed a little.

If this was just a normal night in normal lives, they could be here together like this. His hand would be in hers, just like this, and they wouldn't have a care in the world. She'd be afraid of nothing. Her life would be as full and rich and bright as a carnival.

What was wrong with pretending it was, and could be, for just one night?

She climbed into the rocking car beside him, snuggled close. And rose into the sky. Beneath, people swarmed across the grass. Teenagers strutted, older couples strolled, children raced. The scents rose up on the wind, an evocative mix she could have breathed in forever.

The downward rush was fast and exciting, making her hair fly out and her stomach race to catch up. Tilting her head upward, she closed her eyes and prepared for the upward swing.

Of course, he kissed her. She'd wanted that, too, that sweet, innocent meeting of lips as they circled over the high summer grass, with the lights around them a rainbow gleam.

They circled again as the first fireworks spewed gold across a black sky.

"It's beautiful." She settled her head on his shoulder. "Like jewels tossed in the sea. Emeralds, rubies, sapphires."

The colors shot upward, fountained and faded on a booming crash. Below, people applauded and whistled, filled the air with noise. Somewhere a baby wailed.

"He's frightened," she murmured. "It sounds like gunshots, or thunder."

"My father used to have an English setter who'd hide under his bed every Fourth." Cade toyed with her fingers as he watched the show. "Trembled for hours once the fireworks got going."

"It's so loud, scary if you don't know what it is." A brilliant flash of gold and sparkling diamonds erupted as they topped the wheel in a rush. Her heart began to race, her head to throb. It was the noise, that was all. The noise, and the sickening way the car rocked as the Ferris wheel jerked to a halt to unload passengers.

"Bailey?" He drew her closer, watching her face. She was trembling now, her cheeks white, her eyes dark.

"I'm all right. Just a little queasy."

"We'll be off soon. Just a couple more cars."

"I'm all right." But the lights flashed again, shattering the sky. And the image rolled into her head like thunder.

"He threw up his hands." She managed a whisper. She couldn't see the lights now, the colored diamonds scattered across the sky. The memory blinded her to everything else. "Threw them up to try to grab the knife. I couldn't scream. I couldn't scream. I couldn't move. There was only the desk light. Just that one beam of light. They're like shadows, and they're screaming, but I can't. Then the lightning flashed. It's so bright, just that one instant, so bright the room's alight with it. And he... Oh, God, his throat. He slashed his throat."

She turned her face into Cade's shoulder. "I don't want to see that. I can't bear to see that."

"Let it go. Just hold on to me and let it go. We're getting off now." He lifted her out of the car, all but carried her across the grass. She was shuddering as if the air had turned icy, and he could hear sobs choking her. "It can't hurt you now, Bailey. You're not alone now."

He wound his way through the field where cars were parked, swore each time a boom of gunpowder made her jerk. She curled up in the seat, rocking herself for comfort while he skirted the hood and got quickly behind the wheel.

"Cry it out," he told her, and turned the key. "Scream if you want to. Just don't let it eat at you like this."

Because he didn't make her feel ashamed, she wept a little, then rested her throbbing head against the seat as he drove down the winding road and back toward the city.

"I keep seeing jewels," she said at length. Her voice was raw, but steady. "Beautiful gemstones. Floods of them. Lapis and opals, malachite and topaz. All different shapes, cut and uncut. I can pick out each one. I know what they are, how they feel in my hand. There's a long piece of chalcedony, smooth to the touch and sword-shaped. It sits on a desk like a paperweight. And this lovely rutilated quartz with silvery threads running through it like shooting stars. I can see them. They're so familiar."

"They make you happy, comfortable."

"Yes, I think they do. When I think of them, when they drift back into my head, it's pleasant. Soothing. There's an elephant. Not this one." She hugged the plush toy against her for comfort. "Soapstone, carved

with a jeweled blanket over its back and bright blue
eyes. He's so regal and foolish.''

She paused a moment, tried to think past the headache pounding in her temples. "There are other
stones, all manner of others, but they don't belong to
me. Still, they soothe. It doesn't frighten me at all to
think of them. Even the blue diamond. It's such a
beautiful thing. Such a miracle of nature. It's amazing, really, that just the right elements, the right min-
erals, the right pressure and the right amount of time
can join together to create something so special.

"They're arguing about them. About it," she continued, squeezing her eyes shut to try to bring it back.
"I can hear them, and I'm angry and feeling righ-
teous. I can almost see myself marching toward that
room where they're arguing, and I'm furious and satisfied. It's such an odd combination of feelings. And
I'm afraid, a little. I've done something... I don't
know."

She strained toward it, fisting her hands. "Something rash or impulsive, or even foolish. I go to the
door. It's open, and their voices echo outside. I go to
the door, and I'm trembling inside. It's not all fear, I
don't think it's just fear. Some of it's temper. I close
my hand over the stone. It's in my pocket, and I feel
better with my hand on it. The canvas bag's there, on
the table by the door. It's open, too, and I can see the
money inside. I pick it up while they shout at each
other."

The lights as they slipped from suburb to city made
her eyes water. She closed them again. "They don't

know I'm there. They're so intent on each other, they don't notice me. Then I see the knife in his hand, the curved blade gleaming. And the other one throws up his hands to grab it. They struggle over it, and they're out of the light now, struggling. But I see blood, and one of the shadows staggers. The other moves in. He doesn't stop. Just doesn't stop. I'm frozen there, clutching the bag, watching. The lights go off, all at once, and it's totally dark. Then the lightning flashes, fills the sky. It's suddenly so bright. When he slices the knife again, over his throat, he sees me. He sees me, and I run.''

"Okay, try to relax." The traffic was murder, choked and impatient. He couldn't take her hand, draw her close, comfort her. "Don't push it now, Bailey. We'll deal with this at home."

"Cade, they're the same person," she murmured, and let out a sound somewhere between a moan and a laugh. "They're the same."

He cursed the clogged streets, hunted for an opening and shot around a station wagon with inches to spare. "The same as what?"

"Each other. They're the same person. But that can't be. I know that can't be, because one's dead and one isn't. I'm afraid I'm going crazy."

Symbols again, he wondered, or truth? "How are they the same?"

"They have the same face."

She carried the stuffed elephant into the house, clutching it to her as if it were a lifeline to reality.

Her mind felt musty, caught between dreams, with a sly headache hovering at the corners waiting to pounce.

"I want you to lie down. I'll make you some tea."

"No, I'll make it. I'll feel better if I'm doing something. Anything. I'm sorry. It was such a wonderful evening." In the kitchen, she set the smiling elephant on the table. "Until."

"It was a wonderful evening. And whatever helps jiggle more pieces in place is worth it. It hurts you." He took her shoulders. "And *I'm* sorry, but you have to get through the rest of it to get where we want to be."

"I know." She lifted a hand to his, squeezed briefly, then turned to put the kettle on the stove. "I'm not going to fall apart, Cade, but I'm afraid I may not be stable." Pressing her fingers to her eyes, she laughed. "Funny statement coming from someone who can't remember her own name."

"You're remembering more all the time, Bailey. And you're the most stable woman I've ever met."

"Then I'm worried about you, too, and your choice of women."

She set cups precisely on their saucers, concentrating on the simple task. Tea bags, spoons, sugar bowl.

In the maple tree, the wood thrush had given over to a whippoorwill, and the song was like liquid silver. She thought of honeysuckle burying a chain-link fence, perfuming the evening air while the night bird called for his mate.

And a young girl weeping under a willow tree.

She shook herself. A childhood memory, perhaps, bittersweet. She thought those vignettes of the past would be coming more quickly now. And she was afraid.

"You have questions." She set the tea on the table, steadied herself and looked at him. "You're not asking them because you're afraid I'll crumble. But I won't. I wish you'd ask them, Cade. It's easier when you do."

"Let's sit down." He pulled out a chair for her, took his time stirring sugar into his tea. "The room has gray carpet, a window, a table by the door. There's a desk lamp. What does the desk look like?"

"It's a satinwood library desk, George III." She set her cup back down with a rattle. "Oh, that was clever. I never expected you to ask about the desk, so I didn't think, and it was just there."

"Concentrate on the desk, Bailey. Describe it for me."

"It's a beautiful piece. The top is crossbanded with rosewood that's inlaid with boxwood lines. The sides, even the kneehole, are inlaid with ovals. One side has a long drawer paneled with false fronts. It opens to shelves. It's so clever. The handles are brass, and they're kept well polished."

Baffled, she stared into her tea. "Now I sound like an antique dealer."

No, he thought, just someone who loves beautiful things. And knows that desk very well.

"What's on the desk?"

"The lamp. It's brass, too, with a green glass shade

and an old-fashioned chain pull. And there are papers, a neat stack of papers aligned with the corner of the desk. A leather blotter is in the center, and a *briefke* sits there.''

"A what?"

"A *briefke,* a little cup of paper for carrying loose stones. They're emeralds, grass green, of varying cuts and carats. There's a jeweler's loupe and a small brass scale. A glass, Baccarat crystal, with ice melting in the whiskey. And…and the knife…" Her breath was strangling, but she forced it free. "The knife is there, carved bone handle, curved blade. It's old, it's beautiful.''

"Is someone at the desk?"

"No, the chair's empty." Easier to look away from the knife, to look somewhere else. "It's a dark, pewter-gray leather. Its back is to the window. There's a storm." Her voice hitched. "There's a storm. Lightning, lashing rain. They're shouting over the thunder.''

"Where are they?"

"In front of the desk, facing each other.''

He pushed her cup aside so that he could take her hand. "What are they saying, Bailey?"

"I don't know. Something about a deposit. Take the deposit, leave the country. It's a bad deal. Too dangerous. His mind's made up.''

She could hear the voices. The words were bouncing out of the static of sound, harsh angry phrases.

Double-crossing son of a bitch.

You want to deal with him, you go ahead. I'm out of it.

Both of us. Together. No backing out.

You take the stones, deal with him. Bailey's suspicious. Not as stupid as you think.

You're not walking out with the money and leaving me twisting in the wind.

"He shoves him back. They're fighting, pushing, shoving, punching. It frightens me how much they hate each other. I don't know how they can despise each other so much, because they're the same."

He didn't want to take her through what had happened next. He had the scene now, the steps. "How are they the same?"

"The same face. Same eyes, dark eyes, dark hair. Everything. Mirror images. Even their voices, the same pitch. They're the same man, Cade. How can they be the same man, unless it didn't happen that way at all—and I've lost not only my memory, but my mind?"

"You're not looking at the simple, Bailey. At the simple and the obvious." His smile was grim, his eyes glowed. "Twins."

"Twins? Brothers?" Everything in her, every part of her being, was repelled. She could only shake her head, and continued to shake it until the movement was frantic. "No, no, no." She couldn't accept that. Wouldn't. "That's not it. That can't be it."

She pushed back from the table abruptly, her chair scraping harshly on the tile. "I don't know what I saw." Desperate now to block it out, she grabbed her cup, slopping tea on the table before she carried it to the sink and dumped it down the drain. "It was dark. I don't know what I saw."

Didn't want to know what she'd seen, Cade concluded. Wasn't ready to know. And he wasn't willing to risk playing analyst until she'd regrouped.

"Put it away for now. It's been a rough day, you need some rest."

"Yes." Her mind was screaming for peace, for oblivion. But she was terrified of sleep, and the dreams that would come with it. She turned, pressed herself against him. "Make love with me. I don't want to think. I just want you to love me."

"I do." He met her seeking mouth with his. "I will."

He led her out of the kitchen, stopping on the way to kiss, to touch. At the base of the stairs, he unbuttoned her blouse, skimmed his hands up her narrow rib cage, then cupped her breasts.

On a broken gasp, she clutched her hands in his hair and dragged his mouth down to hers.

He'd wanted to be gentle, tender. But her lips were wild and desperate. He understood that it was the wild and desperate she needed. And let himself go.

He tore the bra aside, watched the shock and arousal flare in her eyes. When his hands possessed this time, they were greedy and rough.

"There's a lot I haven't shown you." He sought the delicate curve between neck and shoulder. Bit. A lot no one had shown her, he thought with a wild spurt of sheer lust. "You may not be ready."

"Show me." Her head fell back, and her pulse scrambled like frightened birds. And fear was suddenly liberating. "I want you to."

He dragged her slacks down her hips, and plunged his fingers inside her. Her nails bit into his shoulders as she rocked on that swift, stunning peak. The whimper in her throat became a cry that was both fear and joy.

His breath hissed out as he watched her fly up, fly over. The dazed shock in her eyes brought him a dark thrill. She was helpless now, if he wanted her helpless.

And he did.

He peeled away layers of clothes, his hands quick and sure. When she was naked and quivering, his lips curved. He traced his thumbs over her nipples until her eyes fluttered closed.

"You belong to me." His voice was thick, rough, compelling. "I need to hear you say it. For now, you belong to me."

"Yes." She would have told him anything. Promised her soul, if that was what he asked of her. This was no lazy river now, but a flood of heaving sensations. She wanted to drown in them. "More."

He gave more. His mouth raced down her body, then fixed greedily on the core of heat.

She swayed, quaked, exploded. Colors burst in her head—carnival lights and jewels, stars and rainbows. Her back pressed into the railing, and her hands gripped at it for balance while her world spun like a carousel gone mad.

Then pleasure, the sharp edge of it tipped toward pain. At that point, between glory and devastation, her body simply shattered.

He pulled her into his arms, darkly pleased that she was limp. Leaving her clothes where they lay, cradling her, he mounted the steps. His bed this time, he thought with a restless, lustful need to claim her there.

He fell to the bed with her, let the fire inside him rage.

It was unbearable. Glorious. His hands, his mouth, destroyed her, rebuilt her. Sweat dewed her skin, slickening it. And, when he'd dragged his clothes away, slickening his. Her body arched and bucked, straining for more, moving eagerly against each new demand.

When he yanked her to her knees, she wrapped herself around him eagerly, bowing back when his head lowered once more to suckle her breast. And when her head touched the mattress, her body bridged, he buried himself deep inside her.

Her moan was low and throaty, a mindless sound as he gripped her hips, braced them. With his own heart screaming in his chest, he drove them both hard and fast. No thoughts, no doubts, nothing but the hot, frenzied joining.

There was moonlight on her face, glinting in her hair, glowing on her damp skin. Even as his vision grayed, he fixed the picture of her in his mind. Locked it there, as the dark pleasure peaked and he emptied himself into her.

* * *

He waited until he was sure she slept. For a time, he simply watched her, bewitched by her and what they'd brought to each other. No woman he'd touched, no woman who had touched him, had ever reached so deep inside him, held his heart so close and fast.

He'd demanded that she tell him she belonged to him. It was no less true that he belonged to her. The miracle of it humbled him.

He touched his lips to her temple. When he left her, she was sprawled on her stomach, one arm flung out where he had lain beside her. He hoped exhaustion would tranquilize her dreams. He left the door open so that he could hear if she cried out in sleep, or called for him.

He took time to brew a pot of coffee and carried it with him into the library. He gave his computer one grim sneer before booting it up. The clock in the corner chimed midnight, then bonged the half hour before he found his rhythm.

In hardly twice the time it would have taken a ten-year-old hacker, the information he was searching for flashed up on the screen.

Gem experts. The greater metropolitan area.

He scrolled through, keeping his senses alert with caffeine, fumbled for a moment in engaging the printer for hard copy.

Boone and Son.

Kleigmore Diamond Consultants.

Landis Jewelry Creations.

His computer provided him with more detailed information than the phone book. For once he blessed technology. He scanned the data, names, dates, then continued to scroll.

Salvini.

Salvini. His eyes narrowed as he skimmed the data. Appraisers and gemologists. Estate jewelry and antiquities a specialty. Established in 1952 by Charles Salvini, now deceased.

Certified and bonded. Consultants to museums and private collectors. Personalized designs, repairs and remounting. All work done on premises.

A Chevy Chase address, he mused. The location was close enough. The firm was respected, had earned a triple-A rating. Owners Thomas and Timothy Salvini.

T.S., he thought on a quick spurt of excitement. Brothers.

Bingo.

Chapter 10

"Just take your time."

Bailey took a deep breath and struggled to be as calm and precise as Cade wanted. "Her nose is sharper than that. I think."

The police artist's name was Sara, and she was young and patient. Skilled, Bailey had no doubt, or Cade wouldn't have called on her. She sat at the kitchen table with her sketch pad and pencils, a cup of steaming coffee at her elbow.

"More like this?" With a few quick strokes, Sara honed down the nose.

"Yes, I think so. Her eyes are bigger, sort of tilted up."

"Almond-shaped?" Sara whisked the gum eraser over the pencil strokes, adjusted for size and shape.

"I suppose. It's hard to see it all in my head."

"Just give me impressions." Sara's smile was easy and relaxed. "We'll go from there."

"It seems the mouth is wide, softer than the rest of the face. Everything else is angles."

"Quite a face," Cade commented as Sara sketched. "Interesting. Sexy."

As Bailey continued to instruct, he studied the image. Angular face, carelessly short hair with long, spiky bangs, with dark, dramatically arched eyebrows peeking through. Exotic and tough, he decided, and tried to hook a personality with the features.

"That's very close to what I remember." Bailey took the sketch Sara offered. She knew this face, she thought, and looking at it brought competing urges to smile and to weep.

M.J. Who was M.J., and what had they shared?

"You want to take a break?" Cade asked and lowered his hands to Bailey's shoulders to rub away the tension.

"No, I'd like to keep at it. If you don't mind," she said to Sara.

"Hey, I can do this all day. Long as you keep the coffee coming." She held her empty mug up to Cade, with a quick smile that told Bailey they knew each other well.

"You— Ah, it's interesting work," Bailey began.

Sara tossed a long ginger-colored braid behind her back. Her outfit was both cool and casual, denim cutoffs and a plain white tank, the combination straight-up sexy.

"It's a living," she told Bailey. "Computers are

slowly putting me out of business. It's amazing what they can do with imaging. But a lot of cops and P.I.'s still prefer sketches." She took her refilled mug back from Cade. "Parris here, he'll do most anything to avoid a computer."

"Hey, I'm getting the hang of it."

Sara snickered. "When you do, I'll be making my living doing caricatures in bars." She shrugged, sipped, then picked up a fresh pencil. "Want to try for the other?"

"Yes, all right." Telling herself not to focus on just how well Cade and Sara knew each other, Bailey closed her eyes and concentrated.

Grace. She let the name cruise through her mind, bring up the image.

"Soft," she began. "There's a softness to her face. It's very beautiful, almost unbelievably so. It's an oval face, very classic. Her hair's ink black, very long. It sort of spills down her back in loose waves. No bangs, just a flow of dark, thick silk. Her eyes are wide, heavy-lidded and thickly lashed. Laser-blue eyes. The nose is short and straight. Think perfect."

"I'm starting to hate her," Sara said lightly, and made Bailey smile.

"It must be hard to be wildly beautiful, don't you think? People only look at the surface."

"I think I could live with it. How about the mouth?"

"Lush. Full."

"Natch."

"Yes, that's good." Excitement began to drum.

The sketch was coming together quickly. "The eyebrows are a little fuller, and there's a mole beside the left one. Just here," Bailey said, pointing to her own face.

"Now I really hate her," Sara muttered. "I don't want to know if she's got the body to match this face. Tell me she's got Dumbo ears."

"No, I'm afraid not." Bailey smiled at the sketch and felt warm and weepy again. "She's just beautiful. It startles the eye."

"She looks familiar."

At Sara's careless comment, Bailey tensed. "Does she? Really?"

"I'd swear I've seen this face before." Pursing her lips, Sara tapped her pencil against the sketch. "In a magazine, maybe. She looks like someone who'd model—pricey perfume or face cream. You got a million-dollar face, you'd be crazy not to use it."

"A model." Bailey bit her lip, fought to remember. "I just don't know."

Sara tore off the sheet, handed it to Cade. "What do you think?"

"A heart-stopper," he said after a moment. "The gene fairy was in one hell of a good mood when she was born. I can't place it, though, and that's a face no man with a pulse would forget."

Her name is Grace, Bailey told herself. And she's more than beautiful. She's not just a face.

"Good work, Sara." Cade laid the two sketches together on the counter. "Got time for one more?"

Sara took a quick look at her watch. "I've got about a half hour to spare."

"The man, Bailey." Cade crouched down until they were eye to eye. "You know what he looks like now."

"I don't—"

"You do." He said it firmly, though his hands were gentle on her arms. "It's important. Just tell Sara how you see him."

It would hurt, Bailey realized. Her stomach muscles were already clenched at the thought of letting that face back into her head. "I don't want to see him again."

"You want the answers. You want it over. This is a step. You've got to take the steps."

She closed her eyes, shifted. Her head began to throb as she put herself back in that room with the gray carpet and the storm-lashed window.

"He's dark," she said quietly. "His face is long, narrow. It's tight with anger. His mouth is grim with temper. It's thin and strong and stubborn. His nose is slightly hooked. Not unattractive, but strong again. It's a very strong face. His eyes are deep-set. Dark. Dark eyes."

Flashing with fury. There was murder in them. She shuddered, hugged her elbows and fought to concentrate.

"Hollowed cheeks and high forehead. His eyebrows are dark and straight. So's his hair. It's well cut, full at the top, very precisely trimmed around the

ears. It's a very handsome face. The jaw spoils it a
little, it's soft, slightly weak.''

"Is that him, Bailey?" Cade put a hand on her
shoulder again, squeezed lightly in support.

Braced, she opened her eyes and looked at the
sketch. It wasn't precise. It wasn't perfect. The eyes
should be a bit farther apart, the mouth slightly fuller.
But it was enough to have her trembling.

"Yes, it's very like him." Mustering all her control, she rose slowly. "Excuse me," she murmured,
and walked out of the room.

"The lady's terrified," Sara commented, sliding
her pencils back in their case.

"I know."

"Are you going to tell me what kind of trouble
she's in?"

"I'm not sure." Cade dipped his hands in his pockets. "But I'm close to finding out. You did good
work, Sara. I owe you."

"I'll bill you." She gathered her tools and rose.
She kissed him lightly, studied his face. "I don't think
you're going to be calling me up for a night on the
town anymore."

"I'm in love with her," he said simply.

"Yeah, I got that." She shouldered her bag, then
touched his cheek. "I'm going to miss you."

"I'll be around."

"You'll be around," she agreed. "But those wild
and wacky days are over for you, Parris. I like her.
Hope you work it out." With a last wistful smile, she
turned. "I know the way out."

He walked her out anyway, and closing the door, realized he was indeed shutting off a part of his life. The freedom of coming and going as he pleased, with whom he pleased. Late nights in a club, with the prospect of friendly, unfettered sex to follow. Responsible to no one but himself.

He glanced up the stairs. She was up there. Responsibility, stability, commitment. One woman from now throughout the rest of his life—a troubled woman, one who had yet to say the words he needed to hear, to make the promises he needed made.

He could still walk away, and she wouldn't blame him. In fact, he was sure that was exactly what she'd expected. It made him wonder who had left her before.

With a shake of his head, he climbed the stairs to her without the slightest regret.

She was standing in the bedroom, looking out the window. Her hands were clasped in front of her, her back was to the door.

"Are you all right?"

"Yes. I'm sorry, I was rude to your friend. I didn't even thank her."

"Sara understands."

"You've known her a long time."

"A few years, yeah."

Bailey swallowed. "You've been together."

Cade lifted a brow, decided against moving to her. "Yeah, we've been together. I've been with other women, Bailey. Women I've liked, cared for."

"Knew." She turned on the word, and her eyes were fierce.

"Knew," he agreed with a nod.

"This is out of sync." She dragged her hands through her hair. "You and me, Cade, it's out of sync with the rest of it. It should never have happened."

"It did happen." He stuck his hands in his pockets, because they'd tensed, wanted to fist. "Are you going to stand there and tell me you're upset because you've met a woman I've slept with? Because I didn't come to you the same way you came to me?"

"Blank." The word shot out of her like a bullet. "You didn't come to me blank. You have family, friends, lovers. A life. I have nothing but pieces that don't fit. I don't care if you've slept with a hundred women." Her voice snapped on that, then whispered fiercely on the rest. "It's that you remember them. Can remember them."

"You want me to tell you they don't matter?" His temper began to inch up, nudged by panic. She was pulling back, pulling away. "Of course they mattered. I can't blank out my past for you, Bailey."

"I wouldn't want you to." She covered her face with her hands for a moment as she fought for even a slippery grip on control. She'd made up her mind. Now she just had to be strong enough to follow through. "I'm sorry. Your private life before I came into it isn't my business, or even the point. The point is, you had one, Cade."

"So did you."

"So did I." She nodded, thinking that was precisely what frightened her. "I never would have gotten this close to finding it without you. But I realize I should have gone to the police straightaway. I've only complicated things by not doing so. But that's what I'm going to do now."

"You don't trust me to finish this?"

"That's not the issue—"

"Damn right it's not," he told her. "This isn't about going to the cops. It's about you and me. You think you can walk out of here and away from what's between us." His hands shot out of his pockets, grabbed her arms. "Think again."

"Someone's dead. I'm involved." Her teeth threatened to chatter as she fought to keep her eyes level with his. "And I shouldn't have involved you."

"It's too late for that now. It was too late the minute you walked into my office. You're not shaking me off." When his mouth crushed down on hers, the kiss tasted of frustration and fury. He held her close, blocking any choice, ravaging her mouth until her hands went limp on his shoulders.

"Don't," she managed when he lifted her off her feet. But that, too, was too late. She was pressed beneath him on the bed, every sense scrambling and screaming as his hands streaked over her.

"I don't give a damn what you forget." Eyes dark and reckless, he dragged at her clothes. "You'll remember this."

He spun her out of control, out of time, out of place. There was a wildness and willfulness here that she'd never experienced and couldn't resist. His mouth closed over her breast, stabbing pleasure through her. Even as she sucked in air to moan, his fingers pierced her and drove her ruthlessly to peak.

She cried out, not in alarm, not in protest, but with the staggered thrill of being plunged beyond reason. Her nails bit into his back, her body moved like lightning under his. She opened herself to him recklessly. The only thought in her head was, *Now, now, now.*

He drove himself into her hard and deep, felt her clutch convulsively around him as she flew over the new crest. It was mindless, desperate. It was wrong. It was irresistible.

He gripped her hands in his, watched pleasure chase shock across her face. The animal inside him had broken free, and it clawed at both of them. So his mouth was rough as it savaged hers. And he pistoned himself inside her until she wept out his name and what was left of his mind shattered.

Empty, hollowed out, he collapsed on her. Her body shuddered under his as a catchy whimper sounded in her throat. Her hands lay, palm out and limp, on the rumpled spread. His mind began to clear enough for shame.

He'd never taken a woman so roughly. Never given a woman so little choice. He rolled away from her, stared at the ceiling, appalled by what he'd found inside himself.

"I'm sorry." It was pathetic, that phrase. The uselessness of it scraped at him as he sat up, rubbed his hands over his face. "I hurt you. I'm sorry. There's no excuse for it." And, finding none, he rose and left her alone.

She managed to sit up, one hand pressed to her speeding heart. Her body felt weak, tingly and still pulsingly hot. Her mind remained fuzzy around the edges, even as she patiently waited for it to clear. The only thing she was certain of was that she had just been savaged. Overwhelmed by sensation, by emotion, by him.

It had been wonderful.

Cade gave her time to compose herself. And used the time to formulate his next steps. It was so difficult to think around fury. He'd been angry before. Hurt before. Ashamed before. But when she came down the stairs, looking tidy and nervous, those three emotions threatened to swamp him. "Are you all right?"

"Yes. Cade, I—"

"You'll do what you want." He interrupted her in a voice that was both cool and clipped. "And so will I. I apologize again for treating you that way."

She felt her stomach sink to her knees. "You're angry with me."

"With both of us. I can deal with myself, but first I have to deal with you. You want to walk out."

"It's not what I want." There was a plea for understanding in her voice. "It's what's right. I've made you an accessory to God knows what."

"You hired me."

She let out an impatient breath. How could he be

so blind and stubborn? "It hasn't been a professional relationship, Cade. It barely started as one."

"That's right. It's personal, and you're not walking out on me out of some misguided sense of guilt. You want to walk for other reasons, we'll get into them after this is done. I love you." There was chilly fury over the words that only deepened the emotion behind them. "If you don't, can't or won't love me, I'll have to live with it. But walking out at this point's just not an option."

"I only want—"

"You want to go to the cops." He paused a moment, hooked his thumbs in his front pockets to keep his hands from reaching for her. "That's fine, it's your choice. But meanwhile, you hired me to do a job, and I'm not finished. Whatever your personal feelings, or mine, I intend to finish. Get your purse."

She wasn't sure how to handle him now. Then again, she realized, had she ever known? Still, this cold, angry man standing in front of her was much more of a stranger than the one she had first seen in a cluttered, messy office only days before.

"The appointment at the Smithsonian," she began.

"I've postponed it. We have somewhere else to go first."

"Where?"

"Get your purse," he repeated. "We're taking this next step my way."

He didn't speak on the drive. She recognized some of the buildings. They'd ridden past them before. But when he drove out of D.C. and into Maryland, her nerves began to jump.

"I wish you'd tell me where we're going." The trees were too close to the road, she thought, panicky. Too green, too big.

"Back," he said. "Sometimes you've just got to open the door and look at what's on the other side."

"We need to talk to the curator at the museum." Her throat was closing. She'd have bartered her soul for a glass of water. "We should turn around and go back to the city."

"You know where we're going?"

"No." The denial was sharp, desperate. "No, I don't."

He only flicked a glance at her out of sharp green eyes. "The pieces are there, Bailey."

He turned left, off the main drag, listening to her breathing coming short and labored. Ruthlessly he repressed his instinct to soothe. She was stronger than he'd pretended she was. He could admit that. And she would get through this. He'd help her get through it.

If the place was being watched, he was bringing her out in the open. He had to weigh the possibility of that against doing his job. She'd hired him to solve the puzzle, he reminded himself. And this, he was sure, was the last piece.

She couldn't continue to live in the safe little world he'd provided for her. It was time, for both of them, to move forward.

Setting his jaw, he pulled into the lot at Salvini.

"You know where we are."

Her skin was clammy. In long, restless strokes, she rubbed her damp palms over the knees of her slacks. "No, I don't."

The building was brick, two stories. Old, rather lovely, with tall display windows flanked by well established azaleas that would bloom beautifully in the spring. There was an elegance to the place that shouldn't have made her shudder.

There was a single car in the lot. A BMW sedan, dark blue. Its finish gleamed in the sunlight.

The building stood alone, taking up the corner, while behind it, across a vast parking lot, a trendy strip mall seemed to be doing a brisk holiday business.

"I don't want to be here." Bailey turned her head, refusing to look at the sign that topped the building in large, clear letters.

SALVINI

"They're closed," she continued. "There's no one here. We should go."

"There's a car in the lot," Cade pointed out. "It won't hurt to see."

"No." She snatched her hand away from his, tried to bury herself in the corner of the seat. "I'm not going in there. I'm not."

"What's in there, Bailey?"

"I don't know." Terror. Just terror. "I'm not going in."

He would rather have cut out his heart than force

her to do what he intended. But, thinking of her, he got out of the car, came around to her side, opened the door. "I'll be with you. Let's go."

"I said I'm not going in there."

"Coward." He said it with a sneer in his voice. "Do you want to hide the rest of your life?"

Fury sparkled off the tears in her eyes as she ripped the seat belt free. "I hate you for this."

"I know," he murmured, but took her arm firmly and led her to the building's front entrance.

It was dark inside. Through the window he could see little but thick carpet and glass displays where gold and stones gleamed dully. It was a small showroom, again elegant, with a few upholstered stools and countertop mirrors where customers might sit and admire their choices.

Beside him, Bailey was shaking like a leaf.

"Let's try the back."

The rear faced the strip mall, and boasted delivery and employee entrances. Cade studied the lock on the employee door and decided he could handle it. From his pocket he took out a leather roll of tools.

"What are you doing?" Bailey stepped back as he chose a pick and bent to his work. "Are you breaking in? You can't do that."

"I think I can manage it. I practice picking locks at least four hours a week. Quiet a minute."

It took concentration, a good touch, and several sweaty minutes. If the alarm was set, he figured, it would go off when he disengaged the first lock. It didn't, and he changed tools and started on the second.

A silent alarm wasn't out of the question, he mused as he jiggled tumblers. If the cops came, he was going to have a lot of explaining to do.

"This is insane." Bailey took another step in retreat. "You're breaking into a store in broad daylight. You can't do this, Cade."

"Did it," he said with some satisfaction as the last tumbler fell. Fastidiously he replaced his tools in the roll, pocketed them. "An outfit like this ought to have a motion alarm in place, as well."

He stepped through the door. In the dim light, he saw the alarm box beside the doorway. Disengaged.

He could almost hear another piece fall into place.

"Careless of them," he murmured. "With the way crime pays."

He took Bailey's hand and pulled her inside. "Nobody's going to hurt you while I'm around. Not even me."

"I can't do this."

"You're doing it." Keeping her hand firm in his, he hit the lights.

It was a narrow room, more of an entranceway with a worn wooden floor and plain white walls. Against the left wall were a watercooler and a brass coatrack. A woman's gray raincoat hung on one of the hooks.

It had called for thunderstorms the previous Thursday, he thought. A practical woman such as Bailey wouldn't have gone to work without her raincoat. "It's yours, isn't it?"

"I don't know."

"Coat's your style. Quality, expensive, subtle." He checked the pockets, found a roll of breath mints, a short grocery list, a pack of tissues. "It's your handwriting," he said, offering her the list.

"I don't know." She refused to look at it. "I don't remember."

He pocketed the list himself, and led her into the next room.

It was a workroom, a smaller version of the one at Westlake. He recognized the equipment now, and deduced that if he took the time to pick the locks on the drawers of a tall wooden cabinet, he would find loose stones. The flood of gems Bailey had described from her dreams. Stones that made her happy, challenged her creativity, soothed her soul.

The worktable was wiped spotlessly clean. Nothing, not the thinnest chain of gold links, was out of place.

It was, he thought, just like her.

"Someone keeps their area clean," he said mildly. Her hand was icy in his as he turned. There were stairs leading up. "Let's see what's behind door number two."

She didn't protest this time. She was too locked in terror to form the words. She winced as he flooded the stairway with light and drew her up with him.

On the second level, the floors were carpeted in pewter gray. Nausea swam in her stomach. The hallway was wide enough for them to walk abreast, and there were gleaming antique tables set at well-

arranged spots. Red roses were fading in a silver vase.
And the scent of their dying sickened her.

He opened a door, nudged it wider. And knew at
first glance that it was her office.

Nothing was out of place. The desk, a pretty, feminine Queen Anne gleamed with polish and care under
the light coating of weekend dust. On it was a long,
milky crystal, jagged at one end, like a broken blade
of a sword. She'd called it chalcedony, he remembered. And the smooth multiangled rock nearby must
be the rutilated quartz.

On the walls were dreamy watercolors in thin
wooden frames. There was a small table beside a love
seat that was thickly upholstered in rose-toned fabric
and set off with pale green pillows. On the table stood
a small glass vase with drooping violets and pictures
framed in polished silver.

He picked up the first. She was about ten, he
judged, a little gangly and unformed, but there was
no mistaking those eyes. And she'd grown to closely
resemble the woman who sat beside her in a porch
glider, smiling into the camera.

"It's your past, Bailey." He picked up another
photo. Three woman, arms linked, laughing. "You,
M.J. and Grace. Your present." He set the picture
down, picked up another. The man was golden, handsome, his smile assured and warm.

Her future? he wondered.

"He's dead." The words choked out of her, slicing
her heart on the journey. "My father. He's dead. The
plane went down in Dorset. He's dead."

"I'm sorry." Cade set the photo down.

"He never came home." She was leaning against the desk, her legs trembling, her heart reeling as too many images crowded their way inside. "He left on a buying trip and never came back. We used to eat ice cream on the porch. He'd show me all the treasures. I wanted to learn. Lovely old things. He smelled of pine soap and beeswax. He liked to polish the pieces himself sometimes."

"He had antiques," Cade said quietly.

"It was a legacy. His father to him, my father to me. Time and Again. The shop. Time and Again. It was so full of beautiful things. He died, he died in England, thousands of miles away. My mother had to sell the business. She had to sell it when…"

"Take it slow, and easy. Just let it come."

"She got married again. I was fourteen. She was still young, she was lonely. She didn't know how to run a business. That's what he said. She didn't know how. He'd take care of things. Not to worry."

She staggered, caught herself. Then her gaze landed on the soapstone elephant with the jeweled blanket on her desk. "M.J. She gave it to me for my birthday. I like foolish things. I collect elephants. Isn't that odd? You picked an elephant for me at the carnival, and I collect them."

She passed a hand over her eyes, tried to hang on. "We laughed when I opened it. Just the three of us. M.J. and Grace and I, just a few weeks ago. My birthday's in June. June nineteenth. I'm twenty-five."

Her head spun as she struggled to focus on Cade.

"I'm twenty-five. I'm Bailey James. My name's Bailey Anne James."

Gently Cade eased her into a chair, laid his hand on hers. "Nice to meet you."

Chapter 11

"It's mixed up in my head." Bailey pressed her fingers to her eyes. Visions were rocketing in, zooming through, overlapping and fading before she could gain a firm hold.

"Tell me about your father."

"My father. He's dead."

"I know, sweetheart. Tell me about him."

"He—he bought and sold antiques. It was a family business. Family was everything. We lived in Connecticut. The business started there. Our house was there. He—he expanded. Another branch in New York, one in D.C. His father had established the first one, then my father had expanded. His name was Matthew."

Now she pressed her hand to her heart as it swelled and broke. "It's like losing him all over again. He was the center of the world to me, he and my mother. She couldn't have any more children. I suppose they spoiled me. I loved them so much. We had a willow tree in the backyard. That's where I went when my mother told me about the crash. I went out and sat under the willow tree and tried to make him come back.''

"Your mother came and found you?" He was guessing now, prompting her gently through her grief.

"Yes, she came out, and we sat there together for a long time. The sun went down, and we just sat there together. We were lost without him, Cade. She tried, she tried so hard to hold the business together, to take care of me, the house. It was just too much. She didn't know how. She met—she met Charles Salvini.''

"This is his building.''

"It was.'' She rubbed her mouth with the back of her hand. "He was a jeweler, specialized in estate and antique pieces. She consulted with him on some of our stock. That's how it started. She was lonely, and he treated her very well. He treated me very well. I admired him. I think he loved her very much, I really do. I don't know if she loved him, but she needed him. I suppose I did, too. She sold what was left of the antique business and married him.''

"Was he good to you?''

"Yes, he was. He was a kind man. And like my father, he was scrupulously honest. Honesty in business, in personal matters, was vital. It was my mother he wanted, but I came with the package, and he was always good to me.''

"You loved him."

"Yes, it was easy to love him, to be grateful for what he did for me and my mother. He was very proud of the business he'd built up. When I developed an interest in gems, he encouraged it. I apprenticed here, in the summers, and after school. He sent me to college to study. My mother died while I was away in college. I wasn't here. I was away when she died."

"Honey." He gathered her close, tried to soothe. "I'm sorry."

"It was an accident. It happened very fast. A drunk driver, crossed the center line. Hit her head on. That was it." Grief was fresh again, raw and fresh. "Charles was devastated. He never really recovered. He was older than she by about fifteen years, and when she died, he lost interest in everything. He retired, went into seclusion. He died less than a year later."

"And you were all alone?"

"I had my brothers." She shuddered, gripped Cade's hands. "Timothy and Thomas. Charles's sons. My stepbrothers." She let out a broken sob. "Twins." Her hands jerked in his. "I want to go now. I want to leave here."

"Tell me about your brothers," he said calmly. "They're older than you."

"I want to go. I have to get out."

"They worked here," Cade continued. "They took over the business from your stepfather. You worked here with them."

"Yes, yes. They took over the business. I came to

work here when I graduated from Radcliffe. We're family. They're my brothers. They were twenty when their father married my mother. We lived in the same house, we're family.''

"One of them tried to kill you."

"No. No." She covered her face again, refused to see it. "It's a mistake. I told you, they're my brothers. My family. We lived together. We work together. Our parents are dead, and we're all that's left. They're impatient or brusque sometimes, but they'd never hurt me. They'd never hurt one another. They couldn't."

"They have offices here? In this building, on this floor?" She shook her head, but her gaze shifted to the left. "I want you to sit right here. Stay right here, Bailey."

"Where are you going?"

"I need to look." He cupped her face, kept his eyes level with hers. "You know I have to look. Stay here."

She let her head fall back against the cushion, closed her eyes. She would stay. There was nothing she needed to see. Nothing she needed to know. She knew her name now, her family. Wasn't that enough?

But it played back in her head, with an echoing crack of lightning that made her moan.

She hadn't moved when Cade came back into the room, but she opened her eyes. And when she did, she saw it on his face.

"It's Thomas," she said hollowly. "It's Thomas who's dead in his office down the hall."

He didn't wonder that she had blocked out what

she'd seen. The attack had been vicious and violent. To witness the cause of the effect in the room he'd just left would have been horrifying. But to watch, from a few feet away, knowing it was one brother savagely slaying another, would have been unspeakable.

"Thomas," she repeated, and let tears fall. "Poor Thomas. He wanted to be the best in everything. He often was. They were never unkind to me. They ignored me a great deal of the time, as older brothers would, I suppose. I know they resented that Charles left me a part of the business, but they tolerated it. And me."

She paused, looked down at her hands. "There's nothing we can do for him, is there?"

"No. I'll get you out of here." He took her hand, helped her to her feet. "We'll call this in."

"They planned to steal the Three Stars of Mithra."

She stood her ground. She could bear it, she promised herself, and she needed to say it all. "We'd been commissioned to verify and assess the three diamonds. Or I had, actually, since that's my field. I often do consults with the Smithsonian. The stars were going to be part of their gem display. They're originally from Persia. They're very old and were once set in a triangle of gold, held in the open hands of a statue of Mithra."

She cleared her throat, spoke calmly now, focused practical. "He was the ancient Persian god of light and wisdom. Mithraism became one of the major religions of the Roman Empire. He was supposed to have slain the divine bull, and from the bull's dying body sprang all the plants and animals.''

"You can tell me in the car."

He urged her to the door, but she simply couldn't move until she'd said it all. "The religion wasn't brought to Rome until 68 B.C., and it spread rapidly. It's similar to Christianity in many respects. The ideals of brotherly love." Her voice broke, forced her to swallow. "The Three Stars were thought to be a myth, a legend spawned by the Trinity, though some scholars believed firmly in their existence, and described them as symbols of love, knowledge and generosity. It's said if one possesses all three, the combination of these elements will bring power and immortality."

"You don't believe that."

"I believe they're powerful enough to bring about great love, great hate, great greed. I found out what my brothers were doing. I realized Timothy was creating duplicates in the lab." She scrubbed at her eyes. "Maybe he could have hidden something like that from me if he'd been more methodical, more careful, but he was always the more impatient of the two, the more reckless." Now her shoulders slumped as she remembered. "He's been in trouble a few times, for assault. His temper is very quick."

"He never hurt you?"

"No, never. He may have hurt my feelings from time to time." She tried a smile, but it faded quickly. "He seemed to feel that my mother had only married his father so that the two of us could be taken care of. It was partially true, I suppose. So it was always important to me to prove myself.''

"You proved yourself here," Cade said.

"Not to him. Timothy was never one to praise. But he was never overly harsh, not really. And I never thought he or Thomas would be dishonest. Until we were commissioned to assess the Stars.''

"And that was more than they could resist.''

"Apparently. The fakes wouldn't fool anyone for very long, but by the time the stones were found out, my brothers would have the money and be gone. I don't know who was paying them, but they were working for someone.''

She stopped on the stairs, stared down. "He chased me down here. I was running. It was pitch-dark. I nearly fell down these stairs. I could hear him coming after me. And I knew he'd kill me. We'd shared Christmas dinner every year of my life since I was fourteen. And he would kill me, the same horrible way he'd killed Thomas. For money.''

She clutched the railing as she slowly walked down to the lower level. "I loved him, Cade. I loved both of them.'' At the base of the steps, she turned, gestured to a narrow door. "There's a basement down there. It's very small and cramped. There's where I ran. There's a little nook under the steps, with a lattice door. I used to explore the building when I was young, and I liked sitting in that nook, where it was quiet. I'd study the gem books Charles gave me. I don't suppose Timothy knew it was there. If he'd known, I'd be dead.''

She walked into the sunlight.

"I honestly don't remember how long I stayed in there, in the dark, waiting for him to find me and kill me. I don't know how I got to the hotel. I must have walked part of the way, at least. I don't drive to work. I live only a few blocks from here."

He wanted to tell her it was done now, but it wasn't. He wanted to let her rest her head on his shoulder and put it behind her. But he couldn't. Instead, he took her hands, turned her to face him.

"Bailey. Where are the other two stars?"

"The—" She went dead pale, so quickly he grabbed her certain she would faint. But her eyes stayed open, wide and shocked.

"Oh, my God. Oh, my God, Cade, what have I done? He knows where they live. He knows."

"You gave them to M.J. and Grace." Moving fast, he wrenched open the car door. The cops would have to wait. "Tell me where."

"I was so angry," she told him as they sped through afternoon traffic. "I realized they were using me, my name, my knowledge, my reputation, to authenticate the gems. Then they would switch them and leave me—leave the business my stepfather had built—holding the bag. Salvini would have been ruined, after all Charles had done to build it. I owed him loyalty. And, damn it, so did they."

"So you beat them to it."

"It was impulse. I was going to face them down with it, but I wanted the Stars out of reach. At least

I thought they shouldn't all be in one place. As long as they were, they could be taken. So I sent one to M.J. and one to Grace, by different overnight couriers.''

"Dear Lord, Bailey, you put priceless diamonds in the mail?''

She squeezed her eyes shut. "We use special couriers regularly for delivering gems.'' Her voice was prim, vaguely insulted. She'd already told herself she'd been unbelievably rash. "All I could think was that there were two people in the world I could trust with anything. I didn't consider they'd be put in danger. I never realized how far it could go. I was certain that when I confronted my brothers, told them I'd separated the diamonds for safe-keeping and would be making arrangements to have the diamonds delivered to the museum, that would have to be the end of it.''

She hung onto the door as his tires spun around a corner. "It's this building. We're on the third floor. M.J. and I have apartments across from each other.''

She was out of the car before he'd fully stopped, and racing toward the entrance. Cursing, he snatched his keys out of the ignition and sprinted after her. He caught her on the stairs. "Stay behind me,'' he ordered. "I mean it.''

Both the lock and the jamb on apartment 324 were broken. Police tape was slashed across it. "M.J.'' was all she could manage as she pushed at Cade and reached for the knob to M.J.'s apartment.

"There you are, dearie.'' A woman in pink stretch

pants and fluffy slippers scuffed down the hall. "I was getting worried about you."

"Mrs. Weathers." Bailey's knuckles turned white on the knob as she turned. "M.J. What's happened to M.J.?"

"Such a hullabaloo." Mrs. Weathers fluffed her helmet of blond hair and gave Cade a measuring smile. "You don't expect such things in a nice neighborhood like this. The world is going to hell in a handbasket, I swear."

"Where's M.J.?"

"Last I saw, she was running off with some man. Clattering down the steps, swearing at each other. That was after all the commotion. Glass breaking, furniture smashing. Gunshots." She nodded briskly several times, like a bird bobbing for juicy worms.

"Shot? Was M.J. shot?"

"Didn't look shot to me. Mad as a wet hen, and fired up."

"My brother. Was she with my brother?"

"No, indeed. Hadn't even seen this young man before. I'da remembered, I can tell you. He was one tall drink of water, had his hair back in one of those cute little ponytails, and had eyes like steel. Dent in his chin, just like a movie star. I got a good look at him, seeing as he nearly knocked me over."

"When did this happen, Mrs. Weathers?"

She fastened her gaze on Cade's face at the question, beamed and offered a hand. "I don't believe we've been introduced."

"I'm Cade, a friend of Bailey's." He flashed a grin

back at her while impatience twisted his stomach. "We've been away for a few days and wanted to catch up with M.J."

"Well, I haven't seen hide nor hair of her since Saturday, when she went running out. Left the door of her apartment wide open—or I thought she had till I saw it was broken. So I peeked in. Her place was a wreck. I know she's not the housekeeper you are, Bailey, but it was upside down and sideways, and..." She paused dramatically. "There was a man laid out cold on the floor. Big bruiser of a man, too. So I skedaddled back to my apartment and called the police. What else could I do? I guess he'd come to and cleared out by the time they got here. Lord knows I didn't put a toe out the door until the cops came knocking, and they said he was gone."

Cade slipped an arm around Bailey's waist. She was starting to tremble. "Mrs. Weathers, I wonder if you might have an extra key to Bailey's apartment. She left it back at my place, and we need to pick up a few things."

"Oh, is that the way of it?" She smiled slyly, fluffed her hair again and admonished Bailey. "And high time, too. Holing yourself up here, night after night. Now, let's see. I just watered Mr. Hollister's begonias, so I've got my keys right here. Here you are."

"I don't remember giving you my key."

"Of course you did, dearie, last year when you and the girls went off to Arizona. I made a copy, just in case." Humming to herself, she unlocked Bailey's door. Before she could push it open and scoot in, Cade outmaneuvered her.

"Thanks a lot."

"No trouble. Can't imagine where that girl got off to," she said, craning her neck to see through the crack in the door of Bailey's apartment. "I told the police how she was running off on her own steam. Oh, and now that I think about it, Bailey, I did see your brother."

"Timothy," Bailey whispered.

"Can't say which one for sure. They look like clones to me. He came by, let's see." She tapped a finger on her front teeth, as if to jiggle the thought free. "Must have been Saturday night. I told him I hadn't seen you, that I thought you might have taken a holiday. He looked a little perturbed. Let himself right in, then closed the door in my face."

"I didn't realize he had a key, either," Bailey murmured, then realized she'd left her purse behind when she ran. She wondered how foolishly useless it would be to change her locks. "Thank you, Mrs. Weathers. If I miss M.J. again, will you tell her I'm looking for her?"

"Of course, dearie. Now, if you—" She frowned as Cade gave her a quick wink, slid Bailey inside and shut the door in her face.

It was just as well he had. One glance around told him his tidy Bailey didn't usually leave her apartment with cushions ripped open and drawers spilled out.

Apparently Salvini hadn't been content to search the place, he'd wanted to destroy it. "Messy amateur," Cade murmured, running a hand up and down her back.

It was the same madness, she realized. The same violent loss of control she'd seen when he grabbed the antique knife Thomas used for a letter opener off the desk. When he used it.

These were only things, she reminded herself. No matter how dear and cherished, they were only things.

She'd seen for herself just what Timothy could do to people. "I have to call Grace. She'd have gone to Grace if she could."

"Did you recognize who M.J. was with from the description?"

"No. I don't know anyone like that, and I know most of M.J.'s friends." She waded through the destruction of her living room and reached the phone. Her message light was blinking, but she ignored it and hastily punched in numbers. "It's her machine," Bailey murmured, and strained while the throaty voice recited the announcement. Then: "Grace, if you're there, pick up. It's urgent. I'm in trouble. M.J.'s in trouble. I don't know where she is. I want you to go to the police, give them the package I sent you. Call me right away."

"Give her my number," Cade instructed.

"I don't know it."

He took the phone himself, recited it, then handed the receiver back to Bailey.

It was a calculated risk, revealing Bailey's whereabouts, but the diamond was going into safekeeping and he didn't want to put up any impediments to

Grace being able to reach them. "It's life-and-death,
Grace. Don't stay in the house alone. Get to the police. Don't talk to my brother, whatever you do. Don't
let him in the house. Call me, please, please, call
me."

"Where does she live?"

"In Potomac." Bailey told him when he gently
took the receiver away and hung it up. "She may not
be there at all. She has a place up in the country,
western Maryland. That's where I sent the package.
There's no phone there, and only a few people know
she goes there. Other times she just gets in the car
and drives until she sees someplace that suits her. She
could be anywhere."

"How long does she usually stay out of touch?"

"No more than a few days. She'd call me, or M.J."
With an oath, she pounced on the message machine.
The first voice to flow out was Grace's.

"Bailey, what are you up to? Is this thing real? Are
we giving smuggling a try? Look, you know how I
hate these machines. I'll be in touch."

"Four o'clock on Saturday." Bailey hung on to
that. "She was all right at four o'clock on Saturday,
according to the machine."

"We don't know where she called from."

"No, but she was all right on Saturday." She
punched to get the next message. This time it was
M.J.

"Bailey, listen up. I don't know what the hell's
going on, but we're in trouble. Don't stay there, he
might come back. I'm in a phone booth outside some

dive near—'' There was swearing, a rattle. ''Hands off, you son of a—'' And a dial tone.

''Sunday, two a.m. What have I done, Cade?''

Saying nothing, he punched in the next message. It was a man's voice this time. ''Little bitch, if you hear this, I'll find you. I want what's mine.'' There was a sob, choked off. ''He cut my face. He had them slice up my face because of what you did. I'm going to do the same to you.''

''It's Timothy,'' she murmured.

''I figured as much.''

''He's lost his mind, Cade. I could see it that night. Something snapped in him.''

He didn't doubt it, not after what he'd seen in Thomas Salvini's office. ''Is there anything you need from here?'' When she only looked around blankly, he took her hand. ''We'll worry about that later. Let's go.''

''Where?''

''A quiet spot where you can sit down and tell me everything else. Then we'll make a call.''

The park was shady and green. Somehow, the little bench under the spreading trees seemed to block out the punch of the oppressive July heat. It hadn't rained in days, and humidity hung like a cloud of wasps in the air.

''You need to have yourself under control when we go to the cops,'' Cade told her. ''You have to have your mind clear.''

"Yes, you're right. And I need to explain everything to you."

"I'm putting the pieces together well enough. That's what I do."

"Yeah." She looked down at her hands, felt useless. "That's what you do."

"You lost your father when you were ten. Your mother did her best, but didn't have a head for business. She struggled to keep a house, raise a daughter alone and run an antique business. Then she met a man, an older man, successful, competent, financially solvent and attractive, who wanted her and was willing to accept her daughter into his family."

She let out an unsteady breath. "I suppose that's it, cutting to the bottom line."

"The child wants a family, and accepts the stepfather and stepbrothers as such. That's it, too, isn't it?"

"Yes. I missed my father. Charles didn't replace him, but he filled a need. He was good to me, Cade."

"And the stepbrothers' noses were a little out of joint at the addition of a little sister. A pretty, bright, willing-to-please little sister."

She opened her mouth to deny it, then closed it again. It was time to face what she'd tried to ignore for years. "Yes, I suppose. I stayed out of their way. I didn't want to make waves. They were both in college when our parents married, and when they came back and were living at home again, I was off. I can't say we were close, but it seemed— I always felt we were a blended family. They never teased or abused me, they never made me feel unwelcome.''

''Or welcome?''

She shook her head. ''There wasn't any real friction until my mother died. When Charles withdrew into himself, pulled back from life so much, they took over. It seemed only natural. The business was theirs. I felt I'd always have a job with the company, but I never expected any percentage. There was a scene when Charles announced I'd have twenty percent. He was giving them forty each, but that didn't seem to be the point to them.''

''They hassled you?''

''Some.'' Then she sighed. ''They were furious,'' she admitted. ''With their father, with me. Thomas backed off fairly quickly though. He was more interested in the sales-and-accounting end than the creative work, and he knew that was my area of expertise. We got along well enough. Timothy was less content with the arrangement, but he claimed I'd get tired of the routine, find some rich husband and leave it all up to them anyway.''

It still hurt to remember that, the way he'd sneered at her. ''The money Charles left me is in trust. It dribbles out to me until I reach thirty. It's not a great deal, but more than enough. More than necessary. He put me through college, he gave me a home, he gave me a career I love.

''And when he sent me to college, he gave me M.J. and Grace. That's where I met them. We were in the same dorm the first semester. By the second, we were rooming together. It was as if we'd known each other all our lives. They're the best friends I've ever had. Oh, God, what have I done?''

''Tell me about them.''

She steadied herself, and tried. ''M.J.'s restless. She changed her major as often as some women change hairstyles. Took all sorts of obscure courses. She'd bomb tests or ace them, depending on her mood. She's athletic, impatient, generous, fun, tough-minded. She tended bar her last year at college for a lark, claimed she was so good at it she'd have to have her own place. She bought one two years ago. M.J.'s. It's a pub off Georgia Avenue, near the District line.''

''I've missed it.''

''It's kind of a neighborhood bar. Regulars, some Irish music on the weekends. If things get rowdy, she takes care of it herself most of the time. If she can't intimidate or outyell someone, she can drop-kick them around the block. She's got a black belt in karate.''

''Remind me not to cross her.''

''She'd like you. She can take care of herself, that's what I keep telling myself. No one can take care of herself better than M. J. O'Leary.''

''And Grace?''

''She's beautiful, you saw that from the sketch. That's what most people see, and they don't see anything else. She uses that when she likes—despises it, but uses it.''

Watching pigeons flutter and strut, Bailey let the memories come. ''She was orphaned young, younger than I, and was raised by an aunt in Virginia. She was expected to behave, to be a certain way, a certain thing. A Virginia Fontaine.''

"Fontaine? Department stores.''

"Yes, money, lots of old money. At least old enough to have that luster a century or so of prestige provides. Because she was beautiful, wealthy and from a fine family, it was expected that she would be properly educated, associate with the right people and marry well. Grace had other ideas.''

"Didn't she pose for…?'' He trailed off, cleared his throat.

Bailey simply lifted a brow. "For a centerfold, yes, while she was still in college. The Ivy League Miss April. She did it without blinking an eye, with the idea of scandalizing her family and, as she put it, exploiting the exploiters. She came into her own money when she was twenty-one, so she didn't give a damn what her proper family thought.''

"I never saw the picture,'' Cade said, wondering if he should be feeling regret or gratitude, under the circumstances. "But it created quite a stir.''

"That's just what she was after.'' Bailey's lips curved again. "Grace liked creating stirs. She modeled for a while, because it amused her. But it didn't satisfy her. I think she's still looking for what will satisfy her. She works very hard for charities, travels on whims. She calls herself the last of the dilettantes, but it's not true. She does amazing work for underprivileged children, but won't have it publicized. She has tremendous compassion and generosity for the wounded.''

"The bartender, the socialite and the gemologist. An unlikely trio."

It made her smile. "I suppose it sounds that way. We— I don't want to sound odd, but we recognized each other. It was that simple. I don't expect you to understand."

"Who'd understand better?" he murmured. "I recognized you."

She looked up then, met his eyes. "Knowing who I am hasn't solved anything. My life is a mess. I've put my friends in terrible danger, and I don't know how to help them. I don't know how to stop what I've started."

"By taking the next step." He lifted her hand, brushed a kiss over the knuckles. "We go back to the house, get the canvas bag, and contact a pal of mine on the force. We'll find your friends, Bailey."

He glanced up at the sky as clouds rolled over the sun. "Looks like we're finally going to get that rain."

Timothy Salvini swallowed another painkiller. His face throbbed so deeply it was difficult to think. But thinking was just what he had to do. The man who had ordered his face maimed, then ordered it tended by his personal physician, had given him one last chance.

If he didn't find Bailey and at least one of the diamonds by nightfall, there was nowhere on earth he could hide.

And fear was a deeper throb than pain.

He didn't know how it could have gone so horribly

wrong. He'd planned it out, hadn't he? Handled the details when Thomas buried his head in the sand. He was the one who'd been contacted, approached. Because he was the one with the brains, he reminded himself. He was the one who knew how to play the games.

And he was the one who'd made the deal.

Thomas had jumped at it at first. Half of ten million dollars would have set his twin up nicely, and would have satisfied his own craving for real wealth.

Not the dribs and drabs of their business income, however successful the business. But real money, money to dream on.

Then Thomas had gotten cold feet. He'd waited until the eleventh hour, when everything was falling into place, and he'd been planning to double-cross his own flesh and blood.

Oh, he'd been furious to see that Thomas had planned on taking the million-plus deposit and leaving the country, leaving all the risk and the responsibility of pulling everything off on him.

Because he was afraid, Salvini thought now. Because he was worried about Bailey, and what she knew. Grasping little bitch had always been in the way. But he'd have handled her, he'd have taken care of everything, if only Thomas hadn't threatened to ruin everything.

The argument had simply gotten out of control, he thought, rubbing a hand over his mouth. Everything had gotten out of control. The shouting, the rage, the flashing storm.

And somehow the knife had just been there, in his hand. Gripped in his hand, and already slicked with blood before he realized it.

He hadn't been able to stop himself. Simply hadn't been able to stop. He'd gone a little mad for a moment, he admitted. But it had been all the stress, the sense of betrayal, the fury at being duped by his own brother.

And she'd been there. Staring at him with those huge eyes. Staring at him out of the dark.

If not for the storm, if not for the dark, he'd have found her, taken care of her. She'd been lucky, that was all, just lucky. He was the one with the brains.

It wasn't his fault. None of it was his fault.

But he was taking the blame for all of it. His life was on the line because of his brother's cowardice and the schemes of a woman he'd resented for years.

He was certain she'd shipped off at least one of the stones. He'd found the receipt for the courier in the purse she'd left in her office when she fled from him. Thought she was clever, he mused.

She'd always thought she was the clever one. Little Miss Perfect, ingratiating herself with his father, coming back from her fancy college years with honors and awards. Honors and awards meant nothing in business. Shrewdness did. Guts did. Canniness did.

And Timothy Salvini had all three.

He would have had five million dollars, too, if his brother hadn't bumbled and alerted Bailey then lost his nerve and tried to double-cross their client.

Client, he thought, gingerly touching his bandaged

cheek. It was more like master now, but that would change, too.

He would get the money, and the stone, find the others. And then he would run far, and he would run fast. Because Timothy Salvini had looked the devil in the eye. And was smart enough to know that once the stones were in the devil's hand, his minion would be of no more use.

So he was a dead man.

Unless he was smart.

He'd been smart enough to wait. To spend hours waiting outside that apartment building for Bailey to come home. He'd known she would. She was a creature of habit, predictable as the sunrise. And she hadn't disappointed him.

Who would have thought that someone so...ordinary could have ruined all his plans? Separating the stones, shipping them off in different directions. Oh, that had been unexpectedly clever of her. And extremely inconvenient for him.

But his job now was to concentrate on Bailey. Others were concentrating on the other women. He would deal with that in time, but for now his patience had paid off.

It had been so easy, really. The fancy car had pulled up, Bailey had leaped out. And the man had followed, in too much of a hurry to lock the car door. Salvini had located the registration in the glove box, noted the address.

Now he was breaking the window on the rear door of the empty house, and letting himself inside.

The knife he'd used to kill his brother was tucked securely in his belt. Much quieter than a gun, and just as effective, he knew.

Chapter 12

"Mick's a good cop," Cade told Bailey as he pulled into the drive. "He'll listen, and he'll clear away the red tape to get to the answers."

"If I'd gone straight to them—"

"You wouldn't be any farther along than you are now," Cade said, interrupting her. "Maybe not as far. You needed time. What you'd been through, Bailey." It sickened him to think about it. "Give yourself a break." He hissed through his teeth as he remembered how ruthlessly he'd pulled her through the building where it had all happened. "I'm sorry I was so hard on you."

"If you hadn't pushed me, I might have kept backing away from it. Avoiding everything. I wanted to."

"It was catching up with you. It was hurting you." He turned, cupped her face. "But if you hadn't blocked it out, you might have gone straight back to your apartment. Like a homing pigeon, calling in your friends. He would have found you. All of you.''

"He'd have killed me. I didn't want to face that. Couldn't, I suppose. I've thought of him as my brother for over ten years, even defended him and Thomas to M.J. and Grace. But he would have killed me. And them.''

When she shuddered, he nodded. ''The best thing you did for all three of you was to get lost for a while. No one would look for you here. Why would they?''

"I hope you're right.''

"I am right. Now the next step is to bring in the cops, get them to put out an APB on Salvini. He's scared, he's hurting and he's desperate. It won't take them long.''

"He'll tell them who hired him.'' Bailey relaxed a little. "He isn't strong enough to do otherwise. If he thinks he can make some sort of deal with the authorities, he'll do it. And Grace and M.J.—''

"Will be fine. I'm looking forward to meeting them.'' He leaned over, opened her door. Thunder rumbled, making her look up anxiously, and he squeezed her hand. "We'll all go to the pub, toss back a few.''

"It's a date.'' Brightening by the image, she got out, reached for his hand. "When this is over, maybe you can get to know me.''

"Sweetheart, how many times do I have to tell you? I knew you the minute you walked in my door.'' He jingled his keys, stuck one in the lock.

It was blind instinct, and his innate need to protect, that saved his life.

The movement was a blur at the corner of his eye. Cade twisted toward it, shoving Bailey back. The quick jerk of his body had the knife glancing down his arm, instead of plunging into his back.

The pain was immediate and fierce. Blood soaked through his shirt, dripped onto his wrist, before he managed to strike out. There was only one thought in his mind—Bailey.

"Get out!" he shouted at her as he dodged the next thrust of the knife. "Run!"

But she was frozen, shocked by the blood, numbed by the horrid replay of another attack.

It all happened so quickly. She was certain she'd no more than taken a breath. But she saw her brother's face, both cheeks bandaged with gauze, a gouge over his left brow.

Murder in his eyes, again.

He lunged at Cade. Cade pivoted, gripped Timothy's knife hand at the wrist. They strained against each other, their faces close as lovers', the smell of sweat and blood and violence fouling the air.

For a moment, they were only shadows in the dim foyer, their breath coming harsh and fast as thunder bellowed.

She saw the knife inch closer to Cade's face, until the point was nearly under his chin, while they swayed together on the bloody wood of the foyer, like obscene dancers.

Her brother would kill again, and she would stand and watch.

She lunged.

It was a mindless, animal movement. She leaped onto his back, tore at his hair, sobbing, cursing him. The sudden jolt sent Cade stumbling backward, his hand slipping, his vision graying around the edges.

With a howl of pain as she dug her fingers into his wounded face, Salvini threw her off. Her head rapped hard on the banister, sent stars circling in her head, flashing like lightning. But then she was up and back at him like vengeance.

It was Cade who pulled her away, threw her back out of the path of the knife that whistled by her face. Then the force of Cade's leap sent both him and his quarry crashing into a table. They grappled on the floor, panting like dogs. The uppermost thought in Cade's mind was to live long enough to keep Bailey safe. But his hands were slippery with blood and wouldn't keep a firm hold.

Using all his strength, he managed to twist Timothy's knife hand, veering the blade away from his own heart, then pushed away.

When he rolled weakly upright, he knew it was over.

Bailey was crawling to him, sobbing his name. He saw her face, the bruise just blooming on her cheekbone. He managed to lift a hand to it.

"You're supposed to leave the heroics to me." His voice sounded thready, faraway, to his own ears.

"How bad are you hurt? Oh God, you're bleeding

so much." She was doing something with the fire in his arm, but it didn't seem to matter. Turning his head, he looked into Salvini's face. The eyes were on him, dimming but still aware.

Cade coughed his throat clear. "Who hired you, you bastard?"

Salvini smiled slowly. It ended in a grimace. His face was bloody, the bandages torn aside, his breathing thin. "The devil" was all he said.

"Well, say hello to him in hell." Cade struggled to focus on Bailey again. Her brows were drawn together in concentration. "You need your glasses for close work, honey."

"Quiet. Let me stop the bleeding before I call for an ambulance."

"I'm supposed to tell you it's just a flesh wound, but the truth is, it hurts like hell."

"I'm sorry. So sorry." She wanted to lay her head on his shoulder and weep, just weep. But she continued to make a thick pad out of what she'd torn from his shirt and pressed it firmly against the long, deep gash. "I'll call for an ambulance as soon as I finish bandaging this. You're going to be fine."

"Call Detective Mick Marshall. Be sure to ask for him, use my name."

"I will. Be quiet. I will."

"What in the world is going on here?"

The voice made him wince. "Tell me I'm hallucinating," he murmured. "Tell me, and I'm begging you, tell me that's not my mother."

"Good God, Cade, what have you done? Is this blood?"

He closed his eyes. Dimly he heard Bailey, in a firm, no-nonsense voice, order his mother to call an ambulance. And, gratefully, he passed out.

He came to in the ambulance, with Bailey holding his hand, rain pattering briskly on the roof. And again in the ER, with lights shining in his eyes and people shouting. Pain was like a greedy beast biting hunks out of his arm.

"Could I have some drugs here?" he asked, as politely as possible, and went out again.

The next time he surfaced, he was in a bed. He remained still, eyes closed, until he tested the level of pain and consciousness. He gave the pain a six on a scale of ten, but he seemed to be fully awake this time.

He opened his eyes, and saw Bailey. "Hi. I was hoping you'd be the first thing I'd see."

She got up from the chair beside the bed to take his hand. "Twenty-six stitches, no muscle damage. You lost a lot of blood, but they pumped more into you." Then she sat on the edge of the bed and indulged in a good cry.

She hadn't shed a tear since she fought to stop the bleeding as he lay on the floor. Not during the ambulance ride, speeding through the wet streets while lightning and thunder strode across the sky.

Or during the time she spent pacing the hospital corridors, or during the headachy ordeal of dealing with his parents. Not even when she struggled to tell the police what had happened.

But now she let it all out.

"Sorry," she said when she'd finished.

"Rough day, huh?"

"As days go, it was one of the worst."

"Salvini?"

She looked away toward the window where the rain ran wet. "He's dead. I called the police. I asked for Detective Marshall. He's outside waiting for you to wake up, and for the doctors to clear him in." She stood, straightened the sheets. "I tried to tell him everything, to make it clear. I'm not sure how well I did, but he took notes, asked questions. He's worried about you."

"We go back some. We'll straighten it out, Bailey," he told her, and reached for her hand again. "Can you hold up a little longer?"

"Yes, as long as it takes."

"Tell Mick to get me out of here."

"That's ridiculous. You've been admitted for observation."

"I've got stitches in my arm, not a brain tumor. I'm going home, drinking a beer and dumping this on Mick."

She angled her chin. "Your mother said you'd start whining."

"I'm not whining, I'm…" He trailed off, narrowed his eyes as he sat up. "What do you mean, my mother? Wasn't I hallucinating?"

"No, she came over to give you a chance to apologize, which apparently you never do."

"Great, take her side."

"I'm not taking her side." Bailey caught herself, shook her head. Could they actually be having this conversation at such a time? "She was terrified, Cade, when she realized what had happened, that you were hurt. She and your father—"

"My father? I thought he was off fly-fishing in Montana."

"He just got home this morning. They're in the waiting room right now, worried to death about you."

"Bailey, if you have one single ounce of affection for me, make them go away."

"I certainly will not, and you should be ashamed of yourself."

"I'll be ashamed later. I've got stitches." It wasn't going to work. He could see that plainly enough. "All right, here's the deal. You can send my parents in, and I'll square things with them. Then I want to see the doctor and get sprung. We'll talk to Mick at home and square things there."

Bailey folded her arms. "She said you always expect to have your own way." With that, she turned and marched to the door.

It took a lot of charm, arguments and stubbornness, but in just over three hours, Cade was sinking onto his own sofa. It took another two, with the distraction of Bailey fussing over him, to fill Mick in on the events since Thursday night.

"You've been a busy boy, Parris."

"Hey, private work isn't eating doughnuts and drinking coffee, pal."

Mick grunted. "Speaking of coffee." He glanced toward Bailey. "I don't mean to put you out, Miss James."

"Oh." She got to her feet. "I'll make a fresh pot." She took his empty mug and hurried off.

"Smooth, Mick, very smooth."

"Listen." Mick leaned closer. "The lieutenant's not going to be happy with two corpses and two missing diamonds."

"Buchanan's never happy."

"He doesn't like play cops like you on principle, but there's a lot of bad angles on this one. Your lady friend waiting four days to report a murder's just one of them."

"She didn't remember. She'd blocked it out."

"Yeah, she says. And me, I believe her. But the lieutenant…"

"Buchanan has any trouble with it, you send him my way." Incensed, Cade pushed himself up and ignored the throbbing in his arm. "Good God, Mick, she watched one of her brothers murder the other, then turn on her. You go to the scene, look at what she looked at, then tell me you'd expect a civilian to handle it."

"Okay." Mick held up a hand. "Shipping off the diamonds."

"She was protecting them. They'd be gone now, if she hadn't done something. You've got her statement and mine. You know exactly how it went down. She's been trying to complete the circle since she came to me.''

"That's how I see it,'' Mick said after a moment, and glanced down at the canvas bag by his chair. "She's turned everything over. There's no question here about self-defense. He broke a pane out in the back door, walked in, waited for you.''

Mick threaded a hand through his wiry hair. He knew how easily it could have gone down another way. How easily he could have lost a friend. "Thought I told you to put in an alarm.''

Cade shrugged. "Maybe I will, now that I've got something worth protecting.''

Mick glanced toward the kitchen. "She's, ah, choice.''

"She's certainly mine. We need to find M. J. O'Leary and Grace Fontaine, Mick, and fast.''

"We?''

"I'm not going to sit on my butt.''

Mick nodded again. "All we've got on O'Leary is there was a disturbance in her apartment, what looks like a whale of a fight, and her running off with some guy wearing a pony tail. Looks like she's gone to ground.''

"Or is being held there,'' Cade murmured, casting a glance over his shoulder to make certain Bailey was still out of earshot. "I told you about the message on Bailey's recorder.''

"Yeah. No way to trace a message, but we'll put a flag out on her. As for Fontaine, I've got men checking her house in Potomac, and we're hunting down her place up in the mountains. I should know something in a couple hours."

He rose, hefted the bag, grinned. "Meanwhile, I get to dump this on Buchanan, watch him tap dance with the brass from the Smithsonian." He had to chuckle, knowing just how much his lieutenant hated playing diplomat with suits. "How much you figure the rocks are worth?"

"So far, at least two lives," Bailey said as she carried in a tray of coffee.

Mick cleared his throat. "I'm sorry for your loss, Miss James."

"So am I." But she would live with it. "The Three Stars of Mithra don't have a price, Detective. Naturally, for insurance purposes and so forth, the Smithsonian required a professional assessment of market value. But whatever dollar value I can put on them as a gemologist is useless, really. Love, knowledge and generosity. There is no price."

Not quite sure of his moves, Mick shifted his feet. "Yes, ma'am."

She worked up a smile for him. "You're very kind and very patient. I'm ready to go whenever you are."

"Go?"

"To the station. You have to arrest me, don't you?"

Mick scratched his head, shifted his feet again. It was the first time in his twenty-year career that he'd had a woman serve him coffee, then politely ask to be arrested. "I'd have a hard time coming up with the charge. Not that I don't want you to stay available, but I figure Cade's got that handled. And I imagine the museum's going to want to have a long talk with you.''

''I'm not going to jail?''

''Now she goes pale. Sit down, Bailey.'' To ensure that she did, Cade took her hand with his good one and tugged.

''I assumed, until the diamonds were recovered...I'm responsible.''

''Your brothers were responsible,'' Cade corrected.

''I have to go with that,'' Mick agreed. ''I'm going to take a rain check on the coffee. I may need to talk to you again, Miss James.''

''My friends?''

''We're on it.'' He gave Cade a quick salute and left.

''Timothy can't hurt them now,'' she murmured. ''But whoever hired him—''

''Only wants the diamonds, not your friends. Odds are Grace is up in her mountain hideaway, and M.J. is out busting some guy's chops.''

It almost made her smile. ''You're right. We'll hear from them soon. I'm sure of it. I'd know if something had happened to them. I'd feel it.'' She poured a cup of coffee, then left it sitting untouched. ''They're the only family I have left. I suppose they're the only family I've had for a long time. I just pretended otherwise.''

''You're not alone, Bailey. You know that.''

No, she wasn't alone. He was there, waiting. "You should lie down, Cade."

"Come with me."

She turned, caught the fresh cockiness of his grin. "And rest."

"I'm not tired."

Her smile faded, and her eyes went dark and serious. "You saved my life."

He thought of the way she'd leaped onto Salvini's back, biting and scratching like a wildcat. "I'd say it was a toss-up as to who saved whom."

"You saved my life," she said again, slowly. "The minute I walked into yours. I'd have been lost without you. Today, you shielded me, fought for me. Risked your life to protect mine."

"I've always wanted to slay the dragon for the damsel. You gave me the chance."

"It's not white knights or Sam Spade." Her voice went rough with emotion. "It was real blood pouring out of you. My brother who turned a knife on you."

"And you," he reminded her. "You're not responsible for what he did, and you're too smart to believe you are."

"I'm trying to be." She turned away for a moment, until she had her courage in place. "If it had gone the other way, if it had been you who died, who else could I blame? I came to you. I brought this to you."

"It's my job." He rose, winced only a little. "Are you going to have a problem with that? What I do for a living? The risks involved with it?"

"I haven't thought that far." She turned back,

faced him. "What you've done for me comes first. I'll never be able to repay you for a moment of it."

In an impatient movement, he scooped the hair out of his face. "You're going to tick me off here, Bailey."

"No, I'm going to say what I have to say. You believed me, right from the first. You took me into your home. You bought me a hairbrush. Something so simple, hundreds of others would have overlooked it. You listened to me and promised to help. You kept your promise. And today it almost killed you."

His eyes went sharp. "Do you want me to tell you I'd die for you? I suppose I would. Would I kill for you? Without question. You're not a fantasy to me, Bailey. You're what made reality snap into place."

Her heart fluttered into her throat and swelled. He was angry with her again, she noted. His eyes were impatient in his bruised face. His arm was bandaged from elbow to shoulder and had to be painful.

And he was hers, without question, for the taking.

"I guess I'm trying to figure out why."

"You want to be reasonable where reason doesn't fit. It's not a piece of the puzzle, Bailey. It's the whole puzzle." Frustrated, he dragged a hand through his hair again. "Love was the first Star, wasn't it? And so is this."

That simple, she realized. That powerful. Pressing her lips together, she took a step toward him. "I'm Bailey James," she began. "I'm twenty-five and live in Washington, D.C. I'm a gemologist. I'm single."

She had to stop, pace herself before she babbled.

"I'm neat. One of my closest friends says neatness is a religion to me, and I'm afraid she may be right. I like everything in its place. I like to cook, but don't often, as I live alone. I like old movies, especially film noir."

He was grinning at her now, but she shook her head. There had to be more to her than that. "Let me think," she muttered, impatient with herself. "I have a weakness for Italian shoes. I'd rather do without lunch for a month than a nice pair of pumps. I like good clothes and antiques. I prefer buying one good thing than several inferior ones. That same friend calls me a retail snob, and it's true. I'd rather go rock-hounding than visit Paris, though I wouldn't mind doing both."

"I'll take you."

But she shook her head again. "I'm not finished. I have flaws, a lot of flaws. Sometimes I read very late into the night and fall asleep with the light on and the TV going."

"Well, we'll have to fix that."

He stepped toward her, but she stepped back, held up a hand. "Please. I squint without my reading glasses, and I hate wearing them because I'm vain, so I squint quite a lot. I didn't date much in college, because I was shy and studious and boring. My only sexual experience has come about recently."

"Is that so? If you'd shut up, you could have another sexual experience."

"I'm not done." She said it sharply, like a teacher

chastising a rowdy student. "I'm good at my work. I designed these rings."

"I've always admired them. You're so pretty when you're serious, Bailey. I've got to get my hands on you."

"I'm not without ambition," she continued, side-stepping his grab for her. "I intend to be successful in what I do. And I like the idea of making a name for myself."

"If you're going to make me chase you around the sofa, at least give me a handicap. I've got stitches."

"I want to be important to someone. I want to know I matter. I want to have children and cook Thanksgiving dinner. I want you to understand that I've tried to be sensible about this, because that's the way I am. I'm precise and I'm practical and I can be very tedious."

"I've never spent such a boring weekend in my entire life," he said dryly. "I could barely keep my eyes open." When she chuckled, he outmaneuvered her and pulled her into his arms. And swore as pain radiated straight up to his shoulder.

"Cade, if you've opened those stitches—"

"You're so precise and practical, you can sew me back up." He lifted her chin with his fingers, smiled. "Are you finished yet?"

"No. My life isn't going to be settled until M.J. and Grace are back and I know they're safe and the Three Stars are in the museum. I'll worry until then. I'm very good at worrying, but I believe you already know that."

"I'll write it down in case it slips my mind again. Now, why don't you take me upstairs and play doctor?"

"There's one more thing." When he rolled his eyes, she drew in a breath. "I love you very much."

He went very still, and the fingers on her chin tightened. Emotions poured through him, sweet and potent as wine. There might not be stars in her eyes, he thought. But her heart was in them. And it belonged to him.

"Took you long enough to get to it."

"I thought it was the best place to finish."

He kissed her for a long, gentle time. "It's a better place to start," he murmured.

"I love you, Cade," she repeated, and touched her lips to his again. "Life starts now."

Epilogue

One Star was out of his reach, for the time being. He'd known the moment it was placed in the hands of the authorities. He hadn't raged or cursed the gods. He was, after all, a civilized man. He had only sent his quivering messenger away with a single icy stare.

Now, he sat in his treasure room, gliding his finger over the stem of a golden goblet filled with wine. Music poured liquidly through the air, soothing him.

He adored Mozart, and gently followed the strains of the music with his hand.

The woman had caused him a great deal of trouble. Salvini had underestimated her, had claimed she was nothing more than a token, a pet of his late father's. With some brains, of course, and undeniable skill, but no courage. A quiet mouse of a woman, he'd been told, who closed herself off with her rocks and minded her own business.

The mistake had been to trust Salvini's estimation of Bailey James.

But he wouldn't make that mistake again. He chuckled to himself. He wouldn't be required to, as Ms. James and her protector had dealt so finally with Timothy Salvini.

And with that convenience, there was nothing to link him with the stones, with the deaths. And nothing to stop him from completing his plan—with some adjustments, of course. He could be flexible when it was necessary.

Two Stars were still free, still lost or wandering. He could see them if he closed his eyes, pulsing with light, waiting for him to take them, unite them with the third. Embrace their power.

He would have them soon enough. Whoever stood in his way would be removed.

It was a pity, really. There had been no need for violence. No need for a single drop of blood to be spilled. But now that it had, well…

He smiled to himself and drank deep of warm red wine. Blood, he thought, would have blood.

Three women, three stones, three Stars. It was almost poetic. He could appreciate the irony of it. And when the golden triangle was complete, when the Three Stars of Mithra were his alone, and he could stroke them as they sat on the altar, he would think of the women who'd tried to turn his destiny aside.

He would remember them with some fondness, even admiration.

He hoped he could arrange for them all to die poetically.

* * * * * *

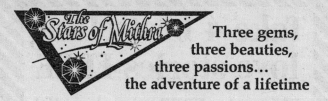

The Stars of Mithra

Three gems,
three beauties,
three passions...
the adventure of a lifetime

SILHOUETTE·INTIMATE·MOMENTS®
brings you a thrilling new series by
New York Times bestselling author

Nora Roberts

Three mystical blue diamonds place three close
friends in jeopardy...and lead them to romance.

In October
HIDDEN STAR (IM#811)
Bailey James can't remember a thing, but she knows
she's in big trouble. And she desperately needs private
investigator Cade Parris to help her live long enough to
find out just what kind.

In December
CAPTIVE STAR (IM#823)
Cynical bounty hunter Jack Dakota and spitfire
M. J. O'Leary are handcuffed together and on the run
from a pair of hired killers. And Jack wants to know
why—but M.J.'s not talking.

In February
SECRET STAR (IM#835)
Lieutenant Seth Buchanan's murder investigation takes
a strange turn when Grace Fontaine turns up alive. But
as the mystery unfolds, he soon discovers the notorious
heiress is the biggest mystery of all.

Available at your favorite retail outlet.

Take 4 bestselling love stories FREE

Plus get a FREE surprise gift!

SHARON SALA

Continues the twelve-book series—36 HOURS— in October 1997 with Book Four

FOR HER EYES ONLY

The storm was over. The mayor was dead. Jessica Hanson had an aching head...and sinister visions of murder. And only one man was willing to take her seriously— Detective Stone Richardson. He knew that unlocking Jessica's secrets would put him in danger, but the rugged cop had never expected to fall for her, too. Danger he could handle. But love...?

For Stone and Jessica and *all* the residents of Grand Springs, Colorado, the storm-induced blackout was just the beginning of 36 Hours that changed *everything!* You won't want to miss a single book.

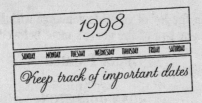

1998

SUNDAY   MONDAY   TUESDAY   WEDNESDAY   THURSDAY   FRIDAY   SATURDAY

Keep track of important dates

Three beautiful and colorful calendars that celebrate some of the most popular trends in America today.

Look for:

Just Babies—a 16 month calendar that features a full year of absolutely adorable babies!

1998 CALENDAR
Just Babies
16 months of adorable bundles of joy!

Hometown Quilts
1998 Calendar
A 16 month quilting extravaganza!

Hometown Quilts—a 16 month calendar featuring quilted art squares, plus a short history on twelve different quilt patterns.

Inspirations—a 16 month calendar with inspiring pictures and quotations.

Inspirations
A 16 month calendar that will lift your spirits and gladden your heart

Steeple Hill™

 HARLEQUIN®

Value priced at $9.99 U.S./$11.99 CAN., these calendars make a perfect gift!

Available in retail outlets in August 1997.   CAL98

Share in the joy of yuletide romance with brand-new
stories by two of the genre's most beloved writers

DIANA PALMER

and

JOAN JOHNSTON

in

LONE STAR CHRISTMAS

Diana Palmer and Joan Johnston share their favorite
Christmas anecdotes and personal stories in this
special hardbound edition.

Diana Palmer delivers an irresistible spin-off of her
LONG, TALL TEXANS series and Joan Johnston crafts an
unforgettable new chapter to **HAWK'S WAY** in this wonderful
keepsake edition celebrating the holiday season. So
perfect for gift giving, you'll want one for yourself...and
one to give to a special friend!

Available in November at your favorite retail outlet!

Only from

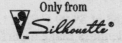

As seen on TV!
Free Gift Offer

With a Free Gift proof-of-purchase from any Silhouette® book,
you can receive a beautiful cubic zirconia pendant.

This gorgeous marquise-shaped stone is a genuine cubic
zirconia—accented by an 18" gold tone necklace.

(Approximate retail value $19.95)

Send for yours today…
compliments of ▼ *Silhouette*®
™

To receive your free gift, a cubic zirconia pendant, send us one original proof-of-purchase, photocopies not accepted, from the back of any Silhouette Romance™, Silhouette Desire®, Silhouette Special Edition®, Silhouette Intimate Moments® or Silhouette Yours Truly™ title available at your favorite retail outlet, together with the Free Gift Certificate, plus a check or money order for $1.65 U.S./$2.15 CAN. (do not send cash) to cover postage and handling, payable to Silhouette Free Gift Offer. We will send you the specified gift. Allow 6 to 8 weeks for delivery. Offer good until December 31, 1997, or while quantities last. Offer valid in the U.S. and Canada only.

Free Gift Certificate

Name: _____

Address: _____

City: _____ State/Province: _____ Zip/Postal Code: _____

Mail this certificate, one proof-of-purchase and a check or money order for postage and handling to: SILHOUETTE FREE GIFT OFFER 1997. In the U.S.: 3010 Walden Avenue, P.O. Box 9077, Buffalo NY 14269-9077. In Canada: P.O. Box 613, Fort Erie, Ontario L2Z 5X3.

FREE GIFT OFFER   084-KFD
ONE PROOF-OF-PURCHASE
To collect your fabulous FREE GIFT, a cubic zirconia pendant, you must include this
original proof-of-purchase for each gift with the properly completed Free Gift Certificate.

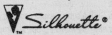